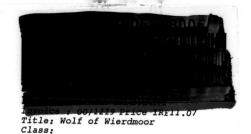

THE WOLF OF WIERDMOOR

KU-489-919

THE WOLF OF WIERDMOOR

Mary Mackie

Chivers Press • Thorndike Press
Bath, England   Thorndike, Maine USA

This Large Print edition is published by Chivers Press, England, and by Thorndike Press, USA.

Published in 1999 in the U.K. by arrangement with the author.

Published in 1999 in the U.S. by arrangement with Laurence Pollinger, Ltd.

U.K. Hardcover   ISBN 0–7540–3805–X (Chivers Large Print)
U.K. Softcover   ISBN 0–7540–3806–8 (Camden Large Print)
U.S. Softcover   ISBN 0–7862–1980–7 (General Series Edition)

The text of this Large Print edition is unabridged.
Other aspects of the book may vary from the original edition.

Set in 16 pt. New Times Roman.

Printed in Great Britain on acid-free paper.

British Library Cataloguing in Publication Data available

Library of Congress Cataloging-in-Publication Data

Mackie, Mary.
        The wolf of Wierdmoor / by Mary Mackie.
            p.   cm.
        ISBN 0–7862–1980–7 (lg. print : sc : alk. paper)
        1. Large type books.   I. Title.
        [PR6063.A2454W65   1999]
        823'.914—dc21
                                                                99–14892

CHAPTER ONE

Alexander was pretending to be asleep. The low lamplight showed his eyes closed a little too tightly and I could hear that his breathing was uneven. He was, I knew, hoping that I would be fooled and would leave him, but after two years I was aware of his tricks. If I left his bedroom he would get up to some mischief. He might even decide to go downstairs and wreck his sister's Coming-Out Ball.

From where I sat quietly in the window corner I could hear the strains of music and occasionally the murmur of voices lifted from the terrace to waft in on the breeze which stirred the lace curtain. Were it not for the odious Alexander I might have slipped along to the gallery and been a hidden spectator. Instead, I had been instructed to watch the boy. Even his doting Mama did not care to have him upsetting her fashionable guests.

The blond curls around the cherubic face were scarcely stirring. Alexander was trying not to breathe, presumably thinking that silence would convince me he was sleeping. It was a war of nerves between this eight-year-old monster and his weary governess.

I wondered who would break first, the boy or myself. The sounds of the Ball taunted me as I kept my vigil, though the boredom was preferable to the two hours of conflict which had preceded it. Alexander had tried every trick he knew which might keep him awake, summon his Mama, or even let him attend the Ball, but after tantrums, feigned illness, chocolate dropped on the counterpane, demands and pleading, he had finally subsided into this pretended sleep.

Clearly on the evening air I heard a church clock chime midnight. The sounds from below continued undiminished, music and laughter, and Alexander was still awake. I had been hoping that tiredness would overcome him, but he had endless endurance.

My own patience was wearing thin. Shaking out my skirts, I went to the door, opened and closed it softly, and remained in the shadows of the room. Instantly the shining curls lifted and the bed-covers heaved. After a quick glance towards the door, the small figure leapt out of bed and went to the open window.

Outside there was a small balcony almost touched by a tree, down which Alexander had climbed only a few days ago. I had no doubt but that the earlier escapade was a trial for this evening, but I was not prepared for the boy's next action. He threw off his nightshirt and, stark naked, prepared to climb through the window.

'Alexander!'

I was across the room in less time than it

2

takes to tell and had him by the arm. He kicked and bit as I lifted him clear of the window and deposited him on the bed with no ceremony.

He lay still, looking at me curiously. 'You knew I wasn't asleep,' he said. 'How did you know?'

'It's my duty to know such things,' I replied shortly. 'You wicked child! Put this nightshirt on at once before I take a hairbrush to you.'

'You wouldn't dare!'

His insolence smote me, grating on my already fraying temper. Tonight was only one instance in a long series of such battles with this wilful child.

Before I had a chance to consider I had grabbed the hairbrush from the dressing-table, turned the boy over, and applied the back of the brush to his unprotected hide. Alexander yelped once and then was silent. I struck four times before I came to my senses and realized what Lady Teignford would say when she heard of it, as she undoubtedly would. Alexander would fly to his Mama and tell her the tale, twisted as only he could make it.

Recklessly, feeling hot and dishevelled, I decided that I did not care. I flung the nightshirt at the boy and watched as he slid into it and lay down, pulling the sheet up.

His voice came clearly up to me as I stood over him, saying, 'You will be sorry you did that, Miss Forrest.'

3

'On the contrary,' I said. 'Your Mama will be extremely angry when I tell her what you were about to do.'

A sly little smirk crossed his face, which boded no good for me. His devilish brain was already laying plans.

He slept then, but I was too exhausted to care about the Ball. I nodded in the chair until, at dawn, Lady Teignford came to look in on her son. She nodded at me, smiled down on the boy as she stroked his tumbled curls, and went away again with a slightly unsteady gait.

In the light of morning my bravado had departed. The loss of my position would be a disaster, especially when Lady Teignford might be reluctant to give me a letter of recommendation. Since she had expressly forbidden me to use corporal punishment, she would no doubt consider that my treatment of her son constituted gross cruelty, not a desirable trait in a governess.

However, Alexander apparently had no intention of running to his Mama. He was all politeness that morning and attended to his lessons with unusual concentration until I was almost convinced that the hairbrush had worked a miracle. Unfortunately for me, the lull was temporary.

Lady Teignford and her daughter were entertaining a visitor that afternoon, a young gentleman who was no doubt dangling after the Teignford fortune, for poor Lucy was a lumpish, ungainly girl whose charms alone would not bring suitors flocking. Alexander, still in his uncanny rôle of angel, joined the party for a while, to show his paces like a pet puppy-dog, and was then banished back to my care.

We had been reading *Oliver Twist*. It was a book which Alexander relished and my rendition of it seemed to hold him enthralled, but this day he began to fidget in his seat so much that my conscience smote me. The poor child might be in pain from the beating I had given him.

Eventually I stopped reading and asked what was wrong.

'Nothing is wrong, thank you, Miss Forrest,' piped Alexander, regarding me with innocent blue eyes. 'Except ... may I be excused for a minute?' He squirmed again to illustrate the reason for this request and I allowed him to leave the room.

He was gone for a very long time. I sat in the quiet school-room listening to the birds in the garden and the clip-clopping rattle of cabs and carriages on the road, but when ten minutes had elapsed I became alarmed. Alexander might be anywhere. Fool that I was to be lulled by his quiescence!

From the corridor I heard Alexander's unsteady young voice raised in song. The sound led me, eventually, to Lady Teignford's boudoir, where my charge was kneeling on the frilled dressing-stool, singing to his reflection in the gilt-framed mirror.

The song stopped abruptly as he caught sight of me and I found myself confronted by the frightening spectacle of a child's face filled by the cold calculation which would have chilled me from an adult. He seemed inhuman in the instant before I shook away the foolish fancy and remembered my duties.

'You have been told not to come into this room, Alexander,' I reminded him.

'My Mama will not mind,' he said, reaching idly to pick up a flagon of perfume and remove the stopper.

I was still in the doorway, uncertain what to do. Alexander was capable of any iniquity. A sweep of his arm would clear the costly bottles and jars from the dressing-table, breaking them and ruining the Brussels carpet, though how he would explain that to his mother was beyond my guessing.

'Put that down, Alexander,' I said quietly. 'Let us go back to the school-room and discover what lies in store for Oliver Twist.'

'I don't wish to. It's more interesting here.' He sniffed delicately at the bottle and smiled at me through the mirror.

Angry with myself for letting the child best me, I decided that he should learn not to disobey me, and advanced determinedly into the room.

When I was still some feet from him,

6

Alexander whirled and flung the flagon of perfume at me. It caught my shoulder and the contents spilled down the front of my grey linen gown while the cut-glass bottle landed with a thud on the thick carpet. A sickening wave of perfume assailed me as I realized that Alexander had used my moment of frozen horror to dodge past me. He was away down the corridor, crying, 'Mama! Mama!'

The wetness was soaking through to my chemise, trickling down my skin. A stain spread from my bodice down the side of my skirt and as I turned helplessly to the door my indignity was completed, for there stood a wide-eyed Lucy with her beau.

Lucy merely gaped in the unattractive way which made her resemble a cod-fish, but the young man's surprise turned quickly to interest as I faced them. I saw his eyes narrow, to blue slits of speculation, though I was too full of the latest disaster to pause and wonder at the thoughts behind that handsome face.

Before any of us had a chance to speak, Lady Teignford appeared in a rustle of silk skirts. The detestable Alexander hung behind, peering at me from the protection of his mother's crinoline.

'You will take a week's notice!' my employer said in tones of outrage before turning to Lucy's companion, fluttering, 'Oh, Mr Cheviot, how can I ever apologize? Such a scene! This reprehensible creature, to whom I have given nothing but kindness, has been trying on my clothes and helping herself to my *parfumerie*.'

'That is not true!' I burst out.

Eyes like stones cut me to size. 'Silence, girl! My son does not tell lies. That he caught you in the act is demonstrated by our noses. You dropped the bottle in your alarm. Come, don't try to deny it.'

I glared furiously at Alexander, who returned my look with a glance of abject fear, cringing against his mother. That, too, was an act. Alexander was afraid of nothing.

'Lady Teignford . . .' I began indignantly.

'Permit me,' broke in Mr Cheviot. 'May I ask a question?'

My employer simpered. 'Of course, dear Mr Cheviot.'

'Am I to understand that the governess has been committing these offences over a period of time?'

'Oh, ages!' said Alexander.

'Then why,' asked Mr Cheviot, 'did you not inform your Mama earlier?'

The boy turned defiant blue eyes upon me. 'She threatened to beat me if I did. And last night . . . last night, she did! Oh, Mama, I have been so afraid. Do please send Miss Forrest away at once.'

Lady Teignford had turned purple with fury. 'Miss Forrest!' she uttered, shocked beyond measure. 'You have dared to . . . Did you lay hands upon my son?'

8

'Not hands,' the child said eagerly. 'A hairbrush. I can show you the bruises, Mama.'

It was something I could not deny. I had no doubt but that Alexander's smooth young rump still bore the marks of the brush and my failure to reply only proved my guilt.

'You are dismissed!' Lady Teignford screeched. 'Go and pack your bags and leave my house at once.'

I straightened my back and walked from the room, knowing that nothing I could say would change the situation. The boy had succeeded in humiliating me, but to have retaliated by telling tales about him would only have made me look smaller. One day Lady Teignford would discover the truth about her angelic son and perhaps then she would think of me and be sorry.

To my mind, Alexander was welcome to his triumph. Retribution could not be far away and I had other things to think about. My future, for example. Where did a disgraced governess find refuge?

That I was no longer a person of any importance was firmly shown to me when Lady Teignford sent the butler to give me the money which was owed to me. Her Ladyship did not wish to see me again, he informed me, and I was to be out of the house by six o'clock.

Although I had no regrets about leaving the unspeakable Alexander, I could have wished that our parting was less precipitous, and less damaging to my professional reputation. After what had happened no respectable family would accept me as a governess. Lady Teignford was sure to tell all her friends what had occurred and I would never have the chance to refute Alexander's lies. I could only hope that my sister would take me in, though it would have to be a temporary arrangement as her husband had no liking for me, nor I for him. Perhaps, though, she would be glad of someone to help her take care of her three small children, for she had written that she was to have another baby and was finding farm life hard.

Accordingly, it was with great disquiet that I quit Siddon House and found myself on the streets of London, with little more money than would buy me a bed for the night and a passage to Kent the next day.

*   *   *

The parks had emptied of the fashionable people out driving, to see and be seen. They would all be taking tea now, prior to dressing for the evening's entertainment. The only people on the streets were hawkers, poorer persons and ragged children begging for pennies.

As I walked along, my valises growing heavier with each step, I thought bitterly of the Ball which I had missed seeing. Such things had no great appeal for me. The Season seemed to encompass much trivia, but how pleasant it would be to attend a grand Ball just once, to sweep down the stairs in embroidered silk, with ringlets falling to my bare white shoulders, meeting the approving gaze of a handsome young gentleman . . .

'Miss Forrest!'

I came out of my imaginings to see that a cab had drawn up beside me and descending from it was the young man who had witnessed my ignominious dismissal from Siddon House—Mr Cheviot.

'Thank goodness I caught you!' he exclaimed.

'Mr Cheviot,' I replied haughtily. 'I can conceive of no reason why you should wish to follow me, unless it is your intention to humiliate me further.'

To my astonishment, he laughed. 'You should have used a little of that spirit on Lady Teignford . . . I am curious. Did you really beat that unpleasant child?'

'I did. But only because he drove me to it. It is not my habit to use violence on my charges.'

'I didn't suppose it was. You have not the look of a harsh governess, and I have heard from elsewhere that Master Alexander is a resourceful liar. You must tell me the true story as we ride.'

'Ride?' I said, with a startled glance at the waiting cab. 'Ride to where, Mr Cheviot?'

'To the house my father has rented for the season. It so happens, my dear Miss Forrest, that my step-mother is anxious to find a congenial companion. And you, I take it, are looking for a post?'

'Why . . . yes, but . . .'

'No buts, Miss Forrest. Come.' He reached out and took my valises, handing them up to the cabby, then bowed to me as he held the cab door open. 'Your carriage, ma'am. At least give us the courtesy of an interview. Lucy has assured me that you speak excellent French, and my poor step-mother is at her wits' end to find such a treasure. Are you so proud that you will forego this opportunity?'

Pride was a thing I could not afford at that moment, though it was highly unusual to hire a companion in such a way. However, I climbed into the cab and Mr Cheviot sat beside me, asking about Alexander in such a disarmingly sympathetic manner that soon I found myself pouring out the story of my two years in the employ of Lord and Lady Teignford.

I could hardly believe my good fortune. How fortuitous that Mr Cheviot had understood my predicament, and that his family needed the services of someone like myself. If Mrs Cheviot accepted me I would be the most unobtrusive companion they had ever seen.

The house where the cab stopped was much smaller than Siddon House, but a smartly-dressed butler opened the door and preceded us up the stairs to the drawing-room. Here, taking tea, were a man and woman, he balding and running to fat, she much younger, with black hair and eyes of lustrous darkness against a skin as pale as milk. Both of them looked up and stared at me.

'What's this?' the older Mr Cheviot grunted, hauling himself with difficulty from the chair. 'Piers . . .'

'Forgive me, father. I couldn't wait to bring Miss Forrest to you. She is in need of employment and I thought immediately of my step-mother's quest for a companion.'

'Indeed?' Small eyes perused me from a ruddy face, as the young man told them briefly of my situation, of what he had witnessed and what had followed.

'Miss Forrest had done nothing to justify her dismissal,' he concluded, 'but because of the malignancy of that child she now finds herself on the streets, with no hope of a favourable reference.'

'H'm,' the older man ruminated, still staring at me thoughtfully. 'What is your background, Miss Forrest?'

'My father was a rector in Kent,' I told him. 'My mother a descendant of French emigrés of noble family. They established a school for the daughters of gentlefolk, at which my sisters and I were educated in divers subjects . . . I speak French fluently, which I understand is a requirement.'

'French?' The woman spoke for the first time, eagerly. *'Vous parlez Francais?'*

'Oui, Madame,' I replied in that language. 'My mother liked to converse in French and it pleased my grandparents when they were alive.'

She turned appealingly to the red-faced man, holding out slender hands. 'Ah, Jonas. This is the one I have been looking for. Please . . .'

Reaching out, he touched her shoulder, giving her a smile of great tenderness. 'A moment, Sophie. I'm not finished with my questions . . . So, Miss Forrest, tell us the rest. Are your family still in Kent?'

'No, sir,' I replied sadly. 'Only my older sister, who is married to a farmer. My parents and younger sister were killed three years ago when the rectory burned to the ground.'

'So you wouldn't object to moving far away? Up North? To Yorkshire, in fact.'

'It has always been my ambition to see more of the country, and if I can be of service to your wife . . .'

'And the child,' Mrs Cheviot said softly, looking up at her husband with glowing eyes. 'The child will need a governess one day, Jonas.'

The portly man straightened with pride, his lips curving as he gazed down on the lovely face upturned to his.

'Very well, my dear. If it will please you, Miss Forrest shall accompany us to Moorhollow.'

I thanked them both with great sincerity and not a little relief. The butler was rung for, to conduct me to my room, but before I left the family I noticed a strange smile on the face of Piers Cheviot. He looked intensely pleased with himself, almost triumphant as he bowed in acknowledgement of my thanks, and though I was momentarily puzzled little did I guess that his gallant rescue of a governess in distress had nothing to do with kindness.

CHAPTER TWO

Just two weeks after I had left Siddon House I sat beside Mrs Cheviot in the carriage as it rolled into Delfdale. Having been brought up in Kent, whose charm is on a smaller scale, I was greatly impressed by the sweeps of empty moorland and the wooded valleys of this part of the country. There seemed to be so much space. Secretly I looked forward to riding out in this wild land and experiencing at first hand the feeling of timelessness which dimly reached me as the carriage swung along. It was an unladylike desire, but I had never been conventional in my nature, much to the despair of my poor parents.

By this time I had learned a great deal about my employers. Mr Cheviot was a wealthy man who owned several mills in Yorkshire and held shares in one of the new railway companies and in a shipping line. He was content to leave much of his business in the hands of managers, while he himself lived a life of ease with his lovely young second wife, whom he had met while on a business visit to France less than two years before. With his son, he made occasional trips to Leeds or Liverpool, but most of the time the family lived at Moorhollow, the country house which Mr Cheviot had had built shortly before the death of his first wife some ten years ago.

As for Piers, I had to concede that my first impression of him as a fortune-hunter must have been incorrect. The young man had no need of a rich wife. I could only conclude that Lady Teignford had invited his attentions to Lucy, which was not to be wondered at, for Piers Cheviot, apart from being his father's heir, was very personable. His fair good looks; his tall, broad-shouldered frame; his impeccable manners and his undeniable charm made him the most eligible of young men, outweighing even the fact that his father's fortune had been earned rather than inherited. Even I, a lowly governess turned companion, could not help but admire the young man. Often as we travelled northwards his eyes had met mine across the carriage and he smiled the disarming smile that intrigued me with its touch of mischief.

Passing through the village of Over Marton we negotiated a bridge which spanned a river of clear, bubbling water. The road climbed gently from the valley bottom, between coppices lush with leaves, and as the carriage swung in a turn I had my first glimpse of the brownstone house that was Moorhollow.

It nestled at the end of a valley, surrounded by trees beneath which the drive led, a monstrosity of jumbled architecture impressive only in its lack of symmetry. I saw a cupola and four ornamental towers, gargoyles and a heavily-studded door. How oddly the place contrasted with Lady Teignford's elegant country home.

As we alighted from the carriage the thunder of hoofbeats made us all turn in some alarm. A young woman on a chestnut mare came galloping towards us at great speed and drew up in a cloud of dust, sawing so savagely at the reins that the horse reared. It was wild-eyed and sweating profusely as it eventually came to earth to stand trembling, but its rider laughed gaily, tossing her head so that the white plume on her hat danced madly.

She cried, 'Welcome home, Papa!'

'You will get yourself killed, Lucinda,' her father replied in a hard voice, dusting down his coat. 'Such hoydenish behaviour is most unbecoming.'

17

Unabashed, the girl slid from her mount, her eyes on me. 'And who is this?'

'This is my companion, Miss Forrest,' Sophie Cheviot said, her quiet voice and pleasant manner utterly feminine beside the strident tones of the posturing girl. 'Miss Forrest, I present my step-daughter Lucinda ... Now let us all go inside. It has been a long and tiring journey.'

*   *   *

The inside of the house was as lavishly decorated as the outside, intricate carvings on the woodwork, paintings in heavy gilded frames, ornaments on small, dark tables, and plants of thick foliage reaching out from painted china tubs. One could well feel cramped in such a place, I thought, but there was always escape on the clean, open moors behind the house.

A pert young maidservant by the name of Molly conducted me to a room on the second floor. It had mahogany furniture, a brass bedstead, and smelled sweetly of lavender. From the window I was pleased that I could see out across the moors, and undulating land of green and purple, with here and there the pale grey of an outcrop of rock.

'That's Wierdmoor, miss,' Molly told me as I stood gazing at that view which was unlike anything I had seen before coming north.

18

'Wierdmoor?' I queried. 'What a strange name.'

'Not really, miss. It's full of bogs and old mine-workings, dangerous even by day. But at night you'd not get anybody in these parts venturing out there. They do say witches meet in Stoney Hollow. People have disappeared on that moor, never to be seen again. Sometimes you see tiny lights dancing, and hear the wolves . . .'

Molly had turned pale at the thought.

'Are there still wolves up here?' I asked, turning again to the window. 'I thought they all died out years ago.'

'They did, miss,' she replied in tones of dread. 'The real animal wolves, that is. But the wolves of Wierdmoor aren't animals . . . They're people! It's true!' she cried as I glanced at her in disbelief. 'They turn to wolves at full moon and come out from their house to roam the moor. They live in a black castle that stands on tall cliffs where the moors meet the sea. A wild, lonely place it is, so I've heard.'

'That's just superstition, Molly,' I said gently. 'Have you seen this castle? Or the wolves?'

Her expression was one of remembered terror. 'I've seen one of them. A big man all dressed in black, with a black cape and a black horse. Most of the people at Moorhollow have seen the Wolf at some time or another, riding on the moor, or just sitting up there on that great black horse, watching the house.'

Fascinating though the tale was, I concluded that it was a blend of folk-lore, superstition and imaginative gossip, with perhaps a kernel of truth somewhere. For myself, I was of a practical nature. Any nonsense about ghosts and hobgoblins had been forcefully subdued by my father, who believed in only one inhuman agency, that being the Devil himself, who was omnipresent and, in our house, most likely to choose me as his tool.

So I dismissed the story with only a lingering mischievous hope that some day I might see for myself this mysterious Wolf whom everyone feared.

Molly brought me a pot of tea and some bread and butter, telling me that dinner would be served in my room at seven o'clock that evening. As had happened during my sojourn with the Teignfords, I found myself hovering in the limbo between masters and servants, being a member of neither class but allied to both. It appeared that the life of a paid companion was to be as lonely as that of a governess, with much more idle time on my hands. And I was not a person who enjoyed being idle.

Shortly after Molly had brought the tray there came another knock and in answer to my summons a young woman peeped timidly round the door.

'Miss Forrest?'

'Yes?' My own tone was questioning, for despite her meek manner her gown of brown silk was not servants' garb. She was a slight girl of perhaps eighteen or nineteen, with hair of pale brown parted in the middle and fastened in a bun at her nape. The softly feminine features of her face could have been pretty were it not for the thick, wire-rimmed glasses which perched on her small nose and made her blue eyes appear huge and distorted.

'Forgive me,' she said, flushing. 'I was so anxious to meet you. My step-Mama said you would not mind if I . . .'

'Your step-Mama?' I queried. 'Are you Miss Lucinda's sister?'

'Yes . . . Oh, I do understand your surprise. Lucinda and I are totally different, are we not? She is so beautiful, so lively. And I . . .' She gestured sadly with her hands, indicating her small, timid self. 'Piers calls me Mouse. It seems an apt name.'

'It seems a very unkind name,' I said. 'I had thought better of your brother.'

A gentle smile lit her eyes. 'He does not mean it unkindly, Miss Forrest. It's just that the contrast is so great between them and me. One would hardly believe that we had the same parents.'

'It would not do for us all to be alike,' I replied. 'What is your real name?'

'Annalie.'

21

'How pretty,' I said sincerely.

'It is, though I always feel that something plainer would be more appropriate. You have a lovely name, too. I thought ...' She hesitated, then rushed on, 'You are not at all what I expected, Miss Forrest.'

'Indeed? And what had you expected, Miss Cheviot?'

'Someone more ... more like myself, I suppose. Miss Barber, who lives in the village, has a companion, but she is much older, and very shy, and plain. You are so pretty. Your hair is ... is redder than new chestnuts.'

'Unfortunately it is not appearance that dictates one's position in life,' I said drily. 'Were it not for your father's kindness in employing me I should be in dire straits indeed. Sometimes I think it would be easier if I *were* of a more retiring nature.'

'You think so?' she asked wistfully. 'Oh no, Miss Forrest. It is a constant agony to be timid, I do assure you. It is torture for me to be in company, especially when Lucinda and Piers are present. I appear in such a bad light beside them. And now there is Sophie, too. I seem fated to be the only unattractive person in the household.'

'You lack only a little confidence,' I said. 'The trick is to hold one's head high and not apologise for being what one is.'

Annalie surveyed me sceptically. 'It is easy for someone like you to say such things. Have you ever needed to apologise for being dull, for stammering with nervousness?'

'No, I have not,' I replied with a smile. 'But I am constantly in trouble from my bad temper and my unfortunate habit of speaking my mind.'

Her lips formed an answering curve. 'I think we shall be friends. You must call me Annalie. Lucinda is Miss Cheviot, not I.'

'I shall be pleased to do so, if you will call me Georgiana.'

'It is settled, then. I cannot tell you how happy I am that you have come to stay here. Perhaps . . . perhaps when my step-Mama does not need you, you could find time to spend with me. Do you think perhaps you might teach *me* to speak French?'

'I see no reason why not,' I said, thinking that if I did so she might take my place as Sophie's companion. Then where would I be? There was the expected baby, of course, but I was a governess, not a nurse, and it would be years before the child required teaching.

Years . . . here at Moorhollow? Perhaps. Perhaps my fate was to grow old in this ugly house among its bleak moors, becoming eventually a companion to Annalie. We were young now but I could picture us both as elderly spinsters, held by the bonds of our differing personalities. The thought sent a shiver down my spine. It was a future too awful to contemplate. There must be something

23

more. There *had* to be.

I dined alone in my room. Outside the wind had risen and it buffeted around the house before streaming on across the moors. Listening to it, I found myself smiling at the tale of wolves. No doubt this wind often howled across the empty land and to the vivid imaginations of country people it might sound like the baying of wolves.

As I had been left to myself ever since arriving at Moorhollow I considered going early to bed, but before I could do so there came a knock on my door and I found myself confronting a sour-faced, elderly maid-servant.

'Madame she wish to see you,' she announced in heavily-accented English. 'Come wiz me.'

I followed her angular figure along passages and down a stairway.

'Are you Mrs Cheviot's maid?' I asked as we reached the lower corridor.

'I am. My name is Babette. I came from France wiz Madame.'

Our skirts whispered along the carpeted passageway until we reached a certain door upon which Babette knocked.

'*Entrez!*' came Sophie's soft voice.

She was propped up in a great muslin-draped four-poster. Her long black hair cascaded over one bare shoulder and the frills of a light nightdress barely hid her swelling breasts.

24

'Ah, Georgie!' she greeted with a smile, slurring the 'gs' so that they sounded like the French 'j'. It was a name she had taken to calling me when we were alone, as I was allowed to use her Christian name in private. '*Cherie*, you have been badly treated. Forgive me. But Jonas has insisted that I rest after the journey. He is anxious about the child, you understand.'

'And you, also,' I said in French. 'Your husband adores you. It is natural that he should be concerned.'

She stretched sensuously, her lips curving. 'It's true. And I had heard such bad reports of Englishmen. They are not cold at all.'

'Especially when they have a beautiful young wife,' I said amusedly. Sophie loved to be flattered and she basked in the adoration of her elderly husband, a fact which she and I both knew and made no secret of knowing. Alone with Sophie I was able to be completely at ease.

'You laugh at me, Georgie,' she said, eyes twinkling. 'But you envy me, yes. I know that it chafes you to be in a position of servitude . . . But yes. Do not argue with me. I have seen it in your eyes. And I shall help you. There are many young men of our acquaintance who would be delighted to have a wife like you. I shall see that you are introduced to the right people. For example, the local curate . . .'

I was dismayed and must have shown it, for

25

she burst into gurgling laughter.

'I am teasing you, *cherie*. No dull preacher for you.'

'If you wish to try your hand at matchmaking,' I replied, 'you have two step-daughters to dispose of. I am not inclined to have a husband chosen for me.'

'Better that than the existence of a governess,' Sophie said. 'As for my step-daughters, I have little hopes of them. Lucinda goes her own way and will come to no good. Of that I am sure. She is too wilful by far. And poor Annalie has not enough colour to catch a man. She turns to stone in company, blushing and stuttering. The young men are anxious to leave her alone and seek the more willing company of Lucinda, who is much *too* willing. You must try to make her more decorous, and bring Annalie out of her shell.'

'*I* must?' I asked in astonishment.

Sophie gave me a knowing smile. 'Of course, my Georgie. You will be good for us all, in many ways. Did you think it was only to speak French that I brought you here?'

'That *was* the impression I received. But I shall be glad to help in any way I can, naturally.'

'You will be grateful? You will remember that I saved you from a fate you brought upon yourself?'

'I thought it was your step-son who saved me,' I said.

'Oh, Piers. Yes. But it was I who pleaded with my husband, was it not? Come, Georgie, do not frown so. You will make lines on your face. I only want to be sure that you will remain my friend. If it were not for my dear Jonas, and now you, who speak in my own language and make me feel at home, I should be very sad here.' She held out a slender white hand, looking at me through her lashes. 'You will be my friend, Georgie?'

'Of course,' I promised, taking her hand in my own. She looked very young and lost there in that huge bed. A stranger, unused to the ways of this bleak land, and pregnant, too. She had been kind to me, made me her confidante. Yes, I was grateful, and growing very fond of her.

'Now I shall sleep in peace,' she said. 'Send Babette to me, will you, Georgie?'

With the pool of lamplight spreading before me, I made my way back to the stairs and was ascending them when I became aware of someone behind me.

'Good evening,' Piers Cheviot said as I glanced round. 'Are you sure you can find your way, Miss Forrest?' He stood at the foot of the stairs, one hand on the banister, his handsome face lifted with a smile.

'I think so, thank you,' I replied.

'That implies some doubt in your mind. Allow me to conduct you.' He was beside me in two strides, relieving me of the lamp, his

27

fingers brushing mine so that I was unsure whether the contact was deliberate or not. As I withdrew my hand Piers smiled down on me, saying pleasantly, 'We can't allow you to get lost, Miss Forrest. This is, after all, your first evening among us.'

'You're very kind, sir,' I said demurely, lowering my eyes so that I could watch where I was stepping.

'Kind?' he repeated in a low voice. 'You mistake me, my dear Miss Forrest. It is merely a clumsy excuse to be with you.'

I looked up at him, astonished by such an assertion.

'You look surprised,' he said. 'Surely you know that you are a beautiful woman?'

'A companion, sir. Beneath your notice, I would have thought.'

Piers' mouth twitched. 'Oh, come, Georgiana. Please do not pretend to be a prim violet. Your spirit is not suited to a humble governess or companion.'

'Perhaps not. But that is what I am. I should be grateful if you would remember it, Mr Cheviot.'

He took my arm as we walked along the corridor, his fingers warm and firm. 'Your station in life is of no importance to me. I see only your beauty and your eyes that can be soft or flashing with fire.'

'Mr Cheviot!' I stopped, disengaging myself from his grasp. Pleased though I was by the

28

compliments it was confusing to hear them from the lips of this young man. 'You should not speak to me in this way.'

'And why not? You have known for some time that I admired you. In the coach, when our eyes met . . . Admit it. You have looked at me as I have looked at you.'

He was very close to me, the lamplight glowing in his eyes and turning his hair to gold.

'Even a lowly governess may look at any man and perhaps admire him,' I replied.

Piers laughed at that. 'You seem determined to humble yourself, Georgiana. You could never be lowly, no matter how you tried.'

'I must not lose sight of reality, sir, even if you choose to ignore it. In my experience there is but one reason why a gentleman such as yourself should pay attention to a female employee and, despite my many faults, I should not welcome such attentions. We may as well have that understood.'

'Oh, quite.' He was trying to look solemn, but a little devil of mischief danced in his eyes. 'You seem to have encountered some ungentlemanly gentlemen. Must I be branded with the faults of others? You forget that I am not a member of the lecherous nobility. My father is a simple mill-owner. And you come from a very respectable family. Do you think I would compromise you?'

'I can see no other reason for your behaviour.'

'Can you not? Is it not possible that I am sincere, with the noblest of intentions?'

'Perhaps. But I am confused by the suddenness of it. I should need time to be convinced.'

'Ah,' he said softly, leaning closer. 'I see that you wish to be wooed. Then forgive my impatience. I shall be the most attentive of lovers until you agree that I am in earnest. But let it not be too long, Georgiana. Constant and faithful I can be with ease, but not patient. No, never that, when I long to make you mine. I have loved you from the first.'

'Love?' I queried.

Piers smiled tenderly into my eyes. 'You heard me right, my Georgiana. Love such as I never hoped to find, from the moment I saw you at Siddon House. Why else do you think I followed you and arranged for you to come here? I could not bear to lose you.'

Breathless with astonishment, I felt his lips on mine, light as the stroke of a butterfly's wing.

'Now here is your door,' he murmured. 'And I must go. Sweet dreams, Georgiana mine. We shall meet tomorrow.'

As he strode away, I turned into my room and stood leaning against the door, my mind in a whirl. The grey years I had so recently envisaged as forming my future now took on a rosier hue. I wondered if Sophie, when speaking of a husband for me, had considered

Piers as a candidate. There was no reason why we should not marry. As he had pointed out, our stations in life were not so very disparate.

I shook myself, ever practical. Dreams were well in their place but one had to view the situation objectively. Only time would tell whether Piers was being honest with me and if he was not then I must not lay up a store of hurt for myself. I had no intention of becoming any man's mistress.

Feeling wide awake, I went across to the window and drew aside the curtain. The wind was still strong, but a bright moon shone down, turning the empty hills to silver. I could see the line of the nearest ridge, not a hundred yards away, curving up and down.

And then I drew a sharp breath, for something broke that gentle line of the hills. A shape. A shadow. It was, I realized with a start, a horseman. Silver light etched the flank of his mount and danced along the billowing cloak that blew out from the man's shoulders. Even as I took note of these details, four great grey shapes came loping up to that waiting figure, giving tongue as they came.

Dogs, I told myself, but some errant twist of my mind amended it—wolves.

CHAPTER THREE

Having no wish to alarm Molly, or to hear more distorted rumours, I refrained from mentioning what I had seen the previous night. The young maid brought my breakfast and, when she returned for the tray, a note from Sophie bidding me to spend the day as I wished, since she had letters to write and would be staying in her room recuperating from the long journey.

The day was bright and warm, the wind having dropped during the night, so I contemplated taking a walk, perhaps with Annalie as a companion. I was intrigued to see the moors and stand where the mysterious horseman had stood, to view the house and try to decide what fascination it held for him.

However, as I reached the entrance hall, I encountered a smiling Piers.

'I hope you slept well,' he said. 'The wind did not disturb you?'

'Not unduly.'

'Or other things? You were not kept awake by the memory of your first experiences at Moorhollow?'

I lifted my head high and met his sparkling gaze. 'I never lose sleep on account of pleasant things.'

'Very commendable. I cannot say the same.

I hardly slept for wondering how I should find you today.'

'I am easy to find,' I replied. 'I rarely indulge in hide and seek.'

Piers smiled, shaking his head. 'Now you are teasing me, Georgiana. I take that as a hopeful sign. I was afraid that cold indifference might have been my lot after my precipitous behaviour. Tell me, how are you going to spend this lovely day?'

'I intend to look for your sister Annalie, in the hopes that she might join me for a walk.'

'A walk?' Piers laughed. 'With Annalie? How dull the prospect sounds. I have a much better idea. Come riding with me. You do ride?'

'I do, but I have no riding habit. And it would be most unseemly for us to ride out alone together.'

He put one finger beneath my chin, blue eyes alight with amusement. 'You still suspect me of base motives, Georgiana. I am deeply wounded. Nothing was further from my mind. Naturally I had intended asking Lucinda to accompany us. And no doubt she could solve the problem of an outfit. She has a cupboard full of riding habits. Now find some other objection.'

'I can see none. Though you have yet to obtain your sister's agreement. She might have other plans.'

'I doubt it. She lives in the saddle. Come, let

us find her.'

Taking my arm, he opened the door of the morning room. The sun streamed in through tall windows, lighting the small figure of Annalie as she sat over a tapestry frame.

'Good morning,' she greeted shyly as Piers released my arm. 'I've been hoping to see you, Georgiana.'

'Where's Lucinda?' Piers asked.

'Gone to her room to change. If you recall, she spilt coffee on her gown.'

'Oh, yes, of course. Then I shall go to ask her about this matter, Miss Forrest, if you will excuse me.' He grinned engagingly as he closed the door behind him.

'Why does Piers want to see Lucinda in such a hurry?' Annalie asked, blinking behind her spectacles. 'They seldom have two polite words to say to each other.'

'He thought she might lend me a riding habit.'

'Are you going out this morning?' Disappointment made her mouth drop. 'I had hoped that we might begin the French lessons. My Papa thinks it is a good idea.'

'Perhaps this afternoon . . .'

'It is my afternoon for visiting. I am taking tea with Miss Barber.'

'Then later. Or tomorrow, if Mrs Cheviot does not require me.'

Annalie had returned her attention to her sewing. 'Please do not worry about me,

Georgiana. No doubt you will find a moment to spare for me sooner or later, when the more interesting members of my family have other things to do.'

'Annalie!' I exclaimed, moving to sit by her side. 'That is not the way of things. If you would like it, I shall tell your brother I have changed my mind.'

'Don't put yourself out on my account,' she said dully. 'I know how overwhelming Piers can be when he chooses. He has great charm and persuasiveness, especially with women. It was only to be expected that he should use it on you.'

'It also happens that I enjoy riding and Mrs Cheviot has given me a free day,' I said, not wishing her to think that my agreement to the outing was entirely because of Piers' influence. 'Why don't you come with us?'

Putting down her needle, she gave me a sad little smile. 'I do not ride. To tell the truth, I am afraid of horses. Really I am the dullest person on earth.'

'I'm sure that is not true. We each have our own particular talent. But I'm sorry to have disapppointed you ... Would it be possible for me to accompany you this afternoon? I should like to meet some of the villagers.'

Annalie brightened. She was the most transparent girl. 'Would you? Oh yes, that would be delightful, Georgiana. And you shall meet Miss Barber's companion, Miss Luce, and see exactly why I was so surprised by you. Poor Miss Luce is even quieter than I, if you can imagine such a person.'

'Easily. And when you smile it is clear that you are not in the least dull. You really should try to do it more often.'

Her smile widened, became soft laughter. 'Dear Georgiana. You make me feel there is hope for me after all. Perhaps some young man may think as you do one day.'

The distorted eyes behind the glasses looked through me, unfocussed except on some bright dream that made her lips go soft.

'Any particular young man?' I asked quietly.

Annalie's eyes fell to the neat tapestry on which she was working, while a scarlet tide suffused her face. 'I know no young men, except for Lucinda's beaus, and none of *them* appeal to me. They are all much too boisterous for my taste.'

'Salving your pride again?' came a sharp voice from the doorway. Lucinda stood there, resplendent in a scarlet habit, with her fair hair caught up in a snood below her jaunty hat. 'My dear Annalie, none of *my* beaus would give you a second glance, however much to your taste he might be. You might be well to take the veil. At least in a nunnery you would not need to find excuses for your deficiencies.'

I stood up to face her, bridling in defence of poor Annalie. 'Many men prefer a quiet, well-mannered woman. Looks do not last. And a sharp tongue soon drives a man to other pursuits.'

The sparkle in Lucinda's eyes reminded me of Piers as she laughed delightedly. 'My tongue knows how to drip honey, Miss Forrest. I never yet lost a beau unless I intended to. How glad I am that you have come. I enjoy a little competition. It makes victory so much sweeter.'

'I can hardly expect to compete with you, Miss Cheviot,' I said quietly.

'You think not? Indeed, you underestimate yourself, *and* the young gentlemen of my acquaintance. You are pretty enough for them to pursue you, though it may not be with the same intentions as they pursue me.'

'Lucinda!' Annalie spoke in tones of disgust. 'Do not speak to Miss Forrest in that way.'

'Why not? She is a paid servant, like any other, though her manner is more haughty than I like to see from a servant.' She watched me through narrowed eyes. 'Do not get above yourself, Miss Forrest. You were hired in a hurry and can be dismissed just as quickly.'

'I am aware of that,' I replied. 'However, it was your father who hired me, and it was not for the purpose of being harangued by you.'

'Are you threatening to run with tales to my father?' Lucinda asked coldly.

'Nothing was further from my mind. I am capable of solving my own problems.'

My adversary licked her lips, enjoying

herself. 'A challenge, is it? Very well, Miss Forrest, I accept. Let us begin by seeing who is the best horsewoman. I have sent one of my old riding habits to your room. It should fit, since it is too big for me. We shall meet at the stables. Piers has already gone to choose a horse for you. I shall see that he finds one with spirit.'

She swept out, leaving the door open.

'Oh dear, Georgiana,' Annalie said worriedly. 'I fear you have made an enemy of Lucinda. Do please be careful. She is so wild.'

'I think I can match her,' I replied. 'Don't worry, Annalie. If she bests me it will not matter.'

But Lucinda, I thought, would not best me. Not on a horse. Truth to tell, I was myself exhilarated by the prospect of matching wits and physical prowess with the spoiled daughter of the house.

The riding habit had a black skirt and green velvet jacket. It had been torn and patched, but that was no more than I had expected. At least it fitted me, and looked well with my red hair.

Piers and Lucinda awaited me in the stable yard with a bay stallion, the chestnut which Lucinda had ridden the previous day, and a mettlesome grey that was prancing nervously on a rein held by a stable-lad.

'How well do you ride?' Piers asked, eyeing the dancing grey. 'We have many quieter mounts.'

'She wants one with spirit,' Lucinda said. 'Dear Miss Forrest, my brother would have had you ride a poor old nag more fitted to the pulling of a plough. I'm sure you prefer *my* choice.'

'She will do admirably,' I said. 'If there is to be some kind of contest I shall need a mount to equal yours.'

Piers looked from one to the other of us, frowning. 'What's this? What contest? Lucinda . . .'

'The challenge has already been taken up,' she said with a toss of the head. 'Do not interfere, brother. This is something between Miss Forrest and myself.'

He turned to me, throwing out a hand. 'Georgiana, I forbid you to take any risks. My sister is . . .'

'Forbid?' Lucinda interrupted. 'Who gave you the right to dictate to Miss Forrest, Piers?'

'Common sense gives me the right,' he said angrily. 'You may risk your neck if you wish, but father would not be pleased if anything happened to Sophie's companion because of your foolery.'

'Oh, Papa!' she replied disdainfully. 'But Papa is not here. And Miss Forrest is a grown woman, capable of understanding the risks—if there are any. Where is the harm in a friendly race? You have entered such contests often enough yourself.'

'With other men!'

'And so?' Lucinda widened her eyes. 'Have men the sole right to enjoyment? Or perhaps you think women incapable of such things. Well, we shall see. Give me a hand up.'

When she was mounted, Piers came to me, linking his hands for my foot. The mare shifted beneath me then stood still, allowing me to stroke her ears.

'You will stay near me, Georgiana,' Piers said in a low voice, his hand on the bridle. 'It is not only for my step-mother's sake that I am anxious. Lucinda is a mad-cap. Don't let her lead you astray.'

'You need have no fear,' I replied. 'I have been riding since I was five years old and have never yet been thrown, even by the most stubborn of horses.'

'Oh, come!' Lucinda cried. 'We've wasted half the morning in this idle chatter.'

She spurred her mare and was away even as Piers vaulted onto the bay. Together we cantered after the fast-receding form of his sister.

It was good to feel a horse under me again, though during my time with Lady Teignford I had had little opportunity for riding and was therefore out of practice. However, I felt that I could still give Lucinda some surprises.

She was waiting for us on the ridge, her face aglow from the attentions of the breeze and from excitement. As we drew near, Piers moved close to me and caught my reins, slowing both horses. His face was solemn as he looked into my eyes.

'Won't you please give up this foolhardy idea? You're new to this country, and to your mount, while Lucinda knows every rabbit-hole. I have no wish to carry you back to Moorhollow in pieces.'

'That will not happen,' I replied. 'I am not entirely foolish, though I admit she has stung me and it would please me to teach her a lesson. I am sorry if you expect me to retreat and make lady-like protestations.'

He shook his head, smiling wryly. 'That would not be in character, my Georgiana. I did not fall in love with a helpless, fainting female. But at least promise to be careful. And watch out for tricks.'

Lucinda proposed that she and I should race to a huge, triangular-shaped boulder which was nearly half a mile away across gently-undulating terrain covered with heather and bracken.

'And the one who returns to Piers first shall be the winner,' she concluded.

'I'm coming, too,' Piers said. 'A straight race to the boulder.'

'No, Piers. You shall stay and judge the end of the race. It is likely to be a close thing, is it not, Miss Forrest?'

'It would seem so,' I replied coolly.

The grey and the chestnut came abreast,

ears pricked, and Lucinda was laughing as she whipped her mount with her crop, making it spring away from us. The grey leaped in pursuit and I bent over her neck, urging her after our flying opponent.

The wind roared in my ears as we thudded across the turf. Faintly I could hear Lucinda laughing and shouting, the while she drew ahead. But I had felt the strength of the grey. Given her head, she could match the chestnut easily, but I let Lucinda remain in front. There were unsuspected holes and rocks which she knew but I did not.

I saw her gather the chestnut for a leap. There was a gully some two feet wide. Checking my mount's stride. I flew across with ease, only two lengths behind. I was smiling to myself, enjoying the wind in my face, the surging of the horse beneath me, and the thrill of the race.

All at once I heard Piers shout from behind me. Glancing round I saw him thundering in pursuit, waving his arm violently. And then I saw that Lucinda had suddenly dragged her mount to the right, not giving me time to follow. There was a pit in a hollow, an old mine working roughly boarded over. I dragged at the reins.

My horse reared, back feet sliding down the incline. Using knees and feet, I hung on. Forehooves pawed the air above me. Then she twisted like a cat and landed sideways, leaping from the hollow in one lithe bound. As I reined her in, Piers reached me.

'Thank God!' he cried, pulling the stallion to a savage halt. 'Georgiana, are you all right?'

My heart was thumping, the breath coming harshly in my lungs. 'Perfectly,' I gasped.

He was beside me, his hand on my wrist. 'I'm a fool!' he said fiercely. 'I had forgotten that old shaft until you were too far away to warn. Forgive me.'

'It is not . . . not for you to apologize,' I said, feeling faint with relief as I looked down into the shallow depression beside me. The boards above the shaft were rotten. If I had tried to ride across, the mare and I would both be dead.

'No.' His voice was grim. 'Lucinda shall apologize. On her knees. If you had come to harm . . .' He stopped sharply. Remembering Lucinda, we had both looked towards the boulder which now commanded the skyline. Beneath it, the chestnut cantered in circles, riderless.

With an oath, Piers dug his heels into the stallion and was away, myself following more slowly on the still-nervous grey. As I topped a small rise I saw Lucinda lying beside a stream, her scarlet habit making a bright splash on the heather.

Sliding from the horse, I hurried to where Piers bent over the still form of his sister. A trickle of bright blood ran down her temple

43

and into the snooded hair.

'I know nothing of doctoring,' Piers said, lifting an anguished face to mine. 'Is she badly hurt?'

'Let me see.'

She was breathing, but further exploration showed me a badly broken leg, the bone protruding through the flesh. Blood poured from the wound.

'Your kerchief,' I snapped to Piers. 'And pass me her riding crop. We need to apply a tourniquet. Quickly, Piers!'

He seemed dazed, but obeyed me. I instructed him to go at once to Moorhollow and fetch some strong men to carry a stretcher. The doctor should be sent for in haste, for the bone had to be set as soon as possible.

Without wasting words, Piers remounted and rode away, flailing the poor stallion in his anxiety. I remained by my patient, holding the crop twisted tightly in the kerchief at Lucinda's knee. Her face was pale as wax, the blood drying on her cheek, her breast rising and falling with the faintest motion.

Around me the moors lay empty beneath the sun. The stream chuckled over stones worn smooth by time and the cold, clear water, and somewhere high above a lark was trilling. Teased by the wind, a lock of hair that had loosened from its coil blew across my eyes and would not be tamed, but I was intent on the unconscious girl, taking note of my surroundings in only a hazy way. She was badly injured, I knew. Yet I had not the knowledge to do any more for her. I could only pray.

The chestnut alerted me. She threw up her head, harness jingling, and set off in the direction of Moorhollow. Even as I lifted my head, the grey sniffed the air and began to back away.

An animal had appeared on the skyline, by the huge rock which had marked the turning point in our unfinished race. It stopped there, poised against the blue of the sky, a slender grey animal with a huge head, pointed muzzle . . . A wolf!

No! I told myself sharply. A dog. Only a big dog.

I wondered why it stood there, but the answer was soon supplied. As if rising from the ground, the hooded head and the shoulders of a man lifted above the ridge, then his body, and his horse. He paused there beside the dog, staring at me, though I could not see his face. It was hidden by the hood of the odd garment he wore, a loose coat with a cowl, fashioned after Arabian clothing. A burnous, black with silver frogging.

Black burnous, black horse, hooded . . .

Slowly, the Wolf began to move towards me, the horse walking delicately, muscles rippling beneath the sheen of its well-groomed coat, with the great dog slinking along behind. I sat

45

fascinated, and a little afraid, though this was no werewolf but a human being who might be of help.

He stopped about ten feet from me, his face a blur in the deep folds of his hood. He sat there in silence, looking at me.

'The young lady is injured,' I said, hoping to still the shivers which played up and down my spine. 'She fell from her horse.'

The stranger made no reply, but lifted his head to look out across the moor beyond me. I saw his hands tighten on the reins, pulling the black stallion round, then he spoke sharply to the dog, dug in his heels and galloped away, his dark cape flying out behind. The dog obediently followed.

Only when the thunder of his hooves had diminished into the stillness did I realize what had alarmed him. There were other horses in the distance, coming this way. A few moments later I saw them myself. Piers and his father, with two of the Moorhollow grooms.

I glanced at the silent Lucinda and beyond her, to the boulder which looked pale in the sunlight. There was no sign of anything, human or otherwise. Yet I had not been imagining things. For the second time, I had seen the Wolf of Wierdmoor.

CHAPTER FOUR

The pall of tragedy crept insidiously through every room of Moorhollow, affecting us all in our different ways. For three days, while Lucinda and the doctor battled for her life, the house was filled with a waiting silence.

Only Sophie retained some of her old gaiety and it was in her company that I spent most of my time. Her husband, fearing that the shock might cause her to lose the baby, had insisted that she remain in her room and though it chafed her to be thus confined she obeyed him, knowing that to have argued would have caused greater distress to a man already half-mad with grief.

'Jonas dotes on his Lucinda,' Sophie told me one day as we sat by the window in her room, sewing tiny garments for the baby. 'Of all his three children she is his favourite, though he chides her for her behaviour. I don't know what he would do if anything should happen to her.'

'Pray God it does not,' I said fervently. 'I hold myself to blame. If I had not encouraged her . . .'

Sophie leaned across and laid a gentle hand on my knee. 'It is in no way your fault, Georgie. Sooner or later, something of the sort was bound to happen. Such a wayward girl. I know that Jonas does not hold you responsible. He knows his own daughter too well for that. And Piers gave him a full account of what happened. Piers will not allow you to be blamed.' She gave me a smiling, sidelong look. 'My step-son was eager to defend you, I understand.'

'No doubt he did not wish to see injustice done,' I said, avoiding her eyes. 'From the plain facts, it would not seem to be my fault, yet if I had only refused to let her prick my stupid pride it might not have happened.'

'Perhaps not on that day. But on some other . . . or in some other way . . . Lucinda courted danger. She cannot but accept that it turned to embrace her. That is all there is to be said about the matter. You are being less than amusing today, and it is your business to amuse me. We must have happy thoughts, for the child's sake.' She stroked her body and her face glowed with the joy of motherhood. 'It will be a boy, I think. I am carrying him very high. That is the sign of a boy-child, is it not?'

'I have heard many varying tales, none of which seem very accurate. Would you prefer a boy?'

Sophie sighed happily. 'A son. Yes. And then a daughter. After that it does not matter.'

'It will be strange for Mr Cheviot to be a father again after such a long interval,' I remarked.

'Not so. It will keep him youthful. He will

enjoy another son, I think.' She smiled, as if at some private secret, her eyes soft with dreams.

'I only hope that by then he is free of worry about Lucinda,' I said.

'He will be. It is six months yet. By that time Lucinda will be back to her old wild ways . . . I shall be glad when everyone ceases to creep about so mournfully. Jonas never listens when I talk, Piers has a grim look which does not suit him, and Annalie resembles a ghost, weeping and wailing if one so much as alludes to Lucinda.'

'I know. But she is very ill, Sophie. You have not seen her.'

'Nor do I wish to. She is being given too much attention already.'

'And you are being ignored?' I queried.

Her mouth tightened, then to my relief she laughed. 'You see me so clearly, Georgie, though it is unkind of you to point out my faults. I am behaving like a child, am I not? But I can't believe that there is real cause for all these long faces.'

'You would if you saw her, lying there so still, her face like parchment. Even her lips are white, and her lovely hair is all damp and tangled. It is very strange to think that it is really Lucinda who only a few days ago was so full of life. The doctor hardly leaves her side.'

'I am being very selfish,' Sophie said, with a downcast expression on her face. 'I would go to see her, but Jonas has forbidden me to go

49

near that room. What do you expect me to do, Georgie? I have my baby to consider. Jonas tells me not to worry, or even think about Lucinda. And here are you, talking of nothing else.'

'I'm sorry ... But look, this little gown is finished.' I held up the dainty garment with its lace and ribbons. 'What do you think?'

'Oh, it's simply beautiful. My baby will look sweet in that, Georgie. You have nimble fingers.'

'I was forced to it by my mother, though it has never been one of my favourite tasks.'

'Nor mine.' Sophie looked ruefully at her pricked fingers. 'However, a lady is expected to sew, it seems. I would rather be dancing, or dining in some great house with amusing people. And you, I don't doubt, would as leave be out riding the moors.'

I looked from the window at the stretch of wild land that was visible above the trees along the valley, tantalizing me by its nearness, and I thought of that strange apparition whom I had met on the day of Lucinda's accident. Who was he? What had been his purpose?

I realized suddenly that Sophie had spoken and was regarding me with amusement.

'Where did you go, Georgie? Out in the sun and wind? With whom, I wonder. Piers?'

'No.' I knew that I was blushing beneath her bright gaze, and rushed on, 'I was thinking of ... Sophie, have you heard of a man they

50

call the Wolf?'

'You have been listening to servant's gossip,' Sophie laughed. 'Babette told me the tale. She believes in many strange things, but I had thought better of *you*. Werewolves on the moors? Nonsense. It's a dismal, unfriendly land, that is all. People invent horrors to amuse themselves.'

'That's what I thought, too,' I said, deciding against telling her of the strange rider in the burnous. No doubt there was some simple explanation. That was usually the case.

'Are you superstitious, Georgie?' Sophie asked. 'You should not be. The only agencies we have to fear are human ones.'

'No, I'm not superstitious. I merely wondered if you had heard the story, or seen anything strange.'

'What is there to see? I have heard the wind howling like demons, but it *was* only the wind. You English are . . .'

She paused and we both turned in surprise as the door flew open and Annalie rushed in. Her hair was dishevelled, her gown crumpled, and tears streamed down her face.

'Oh, Sophie! Georgiana! Forgive me, but . . . Lucinda has awoken. She will recover.'

As I came to my feet, Annalie collapsed on the big four poster, weeping noisily in her relief.

'That is wonderful news,' I said, touching her shoulder. 'Annalie, there is no need to

51

weep now.'

'Hysterics,' Sophie said brusquely. 'Get my smelling salts, Georgie, before she floods my bed.'

We soon managed to calm Annalie and she sat shame-faced, wiping her eyes and apologizing confusedly for bursting in and making a show of herself.

'But I am so glad. I cannot tell you how glad I am. It has been torture to see her lying there so still. I was afraid . . .' She gulped and looked at me appealingly. 'I thought she would die, Georgiana.'

'Not she!' Sophie said.

Annalie stared at her. 'That is unkind. How can you say that? Oh, I know you hate her. You hate her because Papa loves her.'

'My dear girl,' Sophie replied, wide-eyed. 'That is entirely untrue. I should be sad if my husband did not love his own children. Do not impute to me your own emotions.'

'Why . . . what . . .' the girl stammered, lips trembling. 'What do you mean?'

'I mean simply that it is you who hate Lucinda. You are jealous of her. No doubt in your secret heart you wished her dead and now you are overcome by remorse at such wicked thoughts.'

'Sophie!' I exclaimed, putting a protective arm around Annalie.

My employer turned her spiked black gaze upon me. 'Why do you English hide your feelings? It is no sin to hate someone. The sin is in concealing it.'

'I do not hate my sister!' Annalie cried passionately, her hands tearing at a sodden wisp of lace which had been her handkerchief. 'It is not true!'

'Then I am sorry,' Sophie said, putting on a placatory smile. 'However, I am glad to see you defending yourself for once, instead of apologizing for your very existence.'

Brushing me aside, Annalie fled, sobbing, from the room, while I turned angrily to the smiling Sophie.

'Why did you speak to her in that way? She was upset.'

'I spoke only the truth. Perhaps now that she has heard it spoken she will be rid of it. It is bad for her to envy Lucinda as she does. She will never be beautiful or sought-after, but that is not Lucinda's fault. Annalie should realize that. And before you say any more, Georgie, let me remind you that *I* am mistress here. I shall deal with my step-daughters as I choose. It is not your place to interfere.'

I backed away, lowering my eyes, though I was still horrified by what she had done to Annalie. 'I apologize.'

'But we shall not quarrel,' Sophie said lightly. 'You are my friend, Georgie. I need you. Neither of my step-daughters has any love for me. Come and sit down and finish this tedious night-gown for me. We shall have

53

luncheon together, then I shall rest and you shall read to me.'

The following morning I was summoned to the library for an interview with Mr Cheviot. The library was a cold, dark room, panelled in oak and with a large desk and armchairs standing between the bookshelves. It smelled of tobacco smoke and leather, most definitely a man's room.

Mr Cheviot was standing by the window, his fleshy frame outlined by the daylight and as he turned I saw that he was smoking a long-stemmed pipe. I had no idea what this interview portended, though I suspected that Mr Cheviot would upbraid me for my disgraceful behaviour on the day of Lucinda's accident.

'Sit down, Miss Forrest.' His voice, with its North-country accent, sounded flat in my ears, neither hostile nor friendly, so I sat in one of the huge leather chairs and waited.

'No doubt you will understand,' he said, puffing out clouds of fragrant smoke, 'that I have been anxious about my daughter for the past few days. Scarce able to think of ought else, in fact. That is why I have been so long in thanking you for your presence of mind. The doctor assures me that Lucinda's chances of life would have been much less without your prompt action.'

'I did only what anyone would have done,' I replied. 'Indeed, sir, you are very generous, for

54

your daughter might not have been injured if I had not behaved so foolishly. I should have done better to try to restrain her.'

Mr Cheviot sighed, shaking his head. 'No-one can restrain Lucinda when she has her mind set on mischief. And I do not doubt that she did intend mischief—to you, Miss Forrest. She intended that you, and not she, should be the victim of an accident. I assure you I have heard the full story from my son, and I hold you in no way to blame for what happened. It seems to me that it was God's swift retribution on her. I am ashamed that a child of mine could plot such wickedness.'

'Forgive me, Mr Cheviot,' I said earnestly, 'but I cannot believe it was wickedness. Your daughter is a high-spirited girl and I had vexed her. I doubt that she had thought it through. She was merely testing my horsemanship. I do not believe that she intended me real harm. It was more thoughtlessness than viciousness.'

He moved away from the window and stared down at me, his red face wrinkled by a frown. 'Now it is you who are being generous, Miss Forrest. Have you come to know my daughter so well in such a short time?'

'I believe so, sir. She and I are not unlike one another in character. I have done many things myself and only understood the consequences later. I am sure that is what happened. Lucinda saw only the amusement of the test, not the possibilities of my failure.'

'You are a remarkable young woman,' Mr Cheviot told me, seating himself with a creaking of joints behind the desk. He laughed suddenly and slapped his thigh. 'Deuced if you aren't. I never before met a preacher's child with so many varying talents. Horsemanship, doctoring ... How come you know about tending a broken leg, Miss Forrest?'

'The doctor was a near neighbour of ours,' I replied. 'He often took me on his calls and taught me a little about nursing, though my parents were not aware of it. They thought I went with him for the pleasure of riding in his dog-cart. I saw and heard many things of which they would not have approved, I fear, but I believe all knowledge can be useful, even to a woman.'

He nodded his head vigorously. 'Yes. It is a good philosophy, Miss Forrest, and I am especially grateful for it since you may have saved my daughter's life.'

'You're very kind, sir. I am only glad that I was able to do something for her. And if I have behaved badly I beg your forgiveness. It will not occur again if I can prevent it, though I fear my temper is wont to rise unexpectedly and when it does I am not always circumspect. Perhaps I should have confessed as much on our first meeting.'

To my surprise I heard Mr Cheviot give a rumbling laugh. 'Nonsense. I would not change the smallest part of you. You are a

56

splendid companion for my wife. She is always in the best of spirits after talking with you and has only praise for your amiability. It is what she has needed—a true friend. We are both exceedingly glad that we found you. Lady Teignford's loss is our gain, what?' He smiled at me broadly, small eyes almost disappearing in folds of flesh. 'Now run along, my dear. And rest assured that you are welcome in this house.'

Much warmed by his words and his agreeable manner, I rose, bobbed a curtsey and left the library feeling happier than at any time since my arrival at Moorhollow.

Sunlight lay on the floor of the passage, coming from a tall window at the end and making a brightness after the gloom of the library. As I blinked in the sudden change of light I realized that someone was standing there by the window.

'I have been waiting for you,' Piers said with a smile. 'Your face is glowing, Georgiana. Was my father kind?'

'Most kind. I expected to be reprimanded.'

'For what? You merely gave Lucinda the competition she desired. And speaking of my sister, she was asking to see you. May I escort you to her room?'

'If you wish.'

He looked down on me in feigned reproof. 'Still cool with me, Georgiana? I had hoped to see you these past days, but it seems you have been avoiding me.'

'I have been otherwise occupied, as you must have known. Besides, with Lucinda so ill it seemed hardly the appropriate time for dalliance.'

'Dalliance?' Piers' blue eyes widened. 'Is that all you think of me? Georgiana, you are exceeding hard on me. What can I do to convince you I am sincere? Or are you toying with me? Does it amuse you to keep me dangling?'

He was more serious than I had seen him. The laughing, teasing Piers looked positively downcast and my sceptical heart began to thaw.

'Indeed not,' I said quietly. 'I would not willingly cause distress to any living thing. But I don't understand what it is you wish me to say.'

'Only that I have a chance, that you look favourably on me. Or do I cause only revulsion in your heart?'

'I should be extremely hard to please if you did.'

The quick joy on his face made my senses leap in answer. He lifted my hand and kissed it fervently, retaining it tightly between his own.

'I must see you alone,' he said. 'This evening, at ten o'clock, leave the house by the side door. I will meet you there and we can walk together in the night air, without fear of being overheard. If you will not, Georgiana, I swear I shall come to your room.'

'I detect a hint of blackmail in that,' I said lightly. 'Very well. I will come. For a walk.'

'I meant nothing more,' Piers assured me. 'I only ask to be in your company, undisturbed by family or servants ... But more of that when we meet. Tonight you shall know everything that is in my heart. Be ready to give me your answer then.'

He walked beside me, smiling down on me as we made our way to the room where Lucinda lay. Annalie was there, sitting quietly by the bed with her embroidery. She looked up with her quick, shy smile and came to her feet.

'Oh, Georgiana, Lucinda has been asking for you. Will you sit with her while I fetch some more silk? I have completely used all the blue. Look.' She displayed her work, a picture of a ship on curling waves with a motto: May your ship come in full of goodness.

'How neatly you sew,' I said with a sigh. 'I wish I had such a talent for it.'

Annalie blushed with pleasure, and turned to her brother. 'Now, Piers, if you are intending to stay, do please be quiet. Lucinda is not yet strong enough to put up with your teasing.'

'I shall be as quiet as you are, Mouse,' Piers said with an affectionate smile. 'Run along and get your thread.'

As Annalie left, I moved across to the bed. Lucinda was still very pale and her lovely hair had been brushed out across the pillow. In a face that had grown thin from her fight with death, her eyes were deep-shadowed pools.

'I am pleased to see you awake,' I said. 'Are you in much pain?'

Her tongue came out to moisten her blanched lips. 'Not so very much, thank you,' she said with difficulty, her voice little more than a whisper. 'Miss Forrest, I am told I must apologize to you.'

'You have nothing to apologize for,' I replied. 'I might have done the same thing myself, without thinking.'

'Thank you.' Her gaze slid to Piers' face. 'You see, Piers, Miss Forrest understands. I was sure she would bear no malice.'

'All the same,' Piers said, 'it was necessary to tell her you regretted your action. And there is something more you have to say.'

'Oh . . . yes. Miss Forrest, you saved my life. I shall always be grateful.'

I touched the white hand lying on the counterpane. 'Please let us forget the whole matter. I am only sorry you were hurt and hope that you will very soon be well again.'

'It was . . . unfortunate. My own fault entirely. Piers . . . I wish to speak to Miss Forrest alone. A woman's matter that does not concern you.'

'I am gone,' Piers said, sending me a private smile as he went to the door.

Sitting down in the chair vacated by

Annalie, I leaned forward so that Lucinda could see me more easily.

'What is it? I shall be only too pleased to help, if I can.'

'Help?' Her voice was stronger, startling me, and as I stared at her I saw a strange glittering in her eyes.

'Help?' she said again, spitting out the word. 'No-one can help me, Miss Forrest. Did they not tell you? I am crippled. The doctor says I may never walk straight again, let alone ride as I have always done. And it is because of you, Miss Forrest!' I sat up, horrified by the venom in that quiet voice. Her eyes flashed hatred at me.

'Yes, you! If I had not been looking back to see how you fared Velvet would not have stumbled and thrown me. You—with your red hair and your high and mighty ways. You may have all the rest of my family cajoled, but I shall never join them. It was beneath me even to notice you, much less to challenge you to a race as though you were my equal. You are not, and never will be.' Her voice was becoming hoarse and when she stopped she coughed drily, hurting her throat.

'You will feel differently when you are well,' I said, keeping my voice quiet. 'It is your illness that makes you so bitter, and the fever . . .'

'I mean it!' she croaked, and flung out a hand, fastening it about my wrist. 'If I am lamed, you will pay for it. I will teach you to

61

reach above your station.'

Her nails dug into me painfully, so that I had difficulty in remembering that she was ill and should be treated gently. For a few moments we struggled silently, Lucinda gripping me ever tighter and myself trying in vain to loosen her fingers.

Then the door opened and instantly Lucinda's hand relaxed, falling limply to the counterpane. As I clasped my smarting wrist I saw her smile wanly at her sister, the weak invalid again.

'Did you get the silk?'

Annalie smilingly held up the strands of blue. 'Mrs Dewiss had some. How are you feeling? Not tired by talking, I hope.'

'A little,' Lucinda said faintly, closing her eyes. 'But I simply had to thank dear Miss Forrest and tell her how sorry I am for my misdeeds. I could not let another day go by.'

'Of course not.' Annalie smiled warmly at me, her eyes bright behind the thick spectacles. 'She will be easier in her mind now, Georgiana. Thank you for coming.'

'Not at all,' I managed to say pleasantly, and took my leave.

In the corridor I looked ruefully at my ill-used wrist. Lucinda's nails had left a set of four lines on my skin, two of which seeped blood. Weak she might be, physically, but her hatred had a terrifying strength.

CHAPTER FIVE

Although I had easily agreed to meet Piers that night, I did not go without a great deal of thought. He had courted me assiduously since we had come to Moorhollow, but I was still unsure of his real intentions. Experiences in the past, both my own and those of other women I had known, had taught me to be wary in my dealings with men. A woman in my position, if not forewarned, could be easy prey.

It might happen that I should think myself unwise for this night's rendezvous, but wisdom, as my father often told me, was not one of my stronger traits, especially when matched against excitement and adventure. For adventure it was to be preparing to meet a handsome young man in the darkness, and there had been little enough of that commodity in my life.

Tonight I would find out for certain whether he was sincere. If his intentions were immoral he would surely prove it when he had me alone and I would be ready to put an end to his designs. If not—if he really meant what he said—why then I should consider myself a fortunate woman. Who would not?

Promptly at ten o'clock I hurried through the quiet house to the side door and let myself out into the darkness. The moon was on the wane, riding high above a veil of scudding cloud, so that patches of light chased across the hardy grass to the wall and beyond to the moors rising against a black sky. There was a cool breeze blowing and I pulled my pelisse more closely around me, glad of its protection.

'Georgiana!' came Piers' low voice and as I turned to the sound his figure detached itself from the shadows of a buttress. Moonlight played on his fair hair and showed up the white stock at his throat as he held out his hands.

Pulling me close, he kissed my fingers one at a time, his lips burning my flesh as they touched.

'Georgiana! I have been in a fever of anxiety. If you had not come I think I should have gone mad.' He reached for me, but I held him off, my hands against the velvet of his jacket. I could feel the hard muscles beneath, and the thudding of his heart which seemed to match pace with mine.

'A walk, you said,' I reminded him.

Piers groaned. 'You are inhuman, Georgiana. One kiss, I beg you.'

'Alas,' I said softly. 'I fear it might not stop at one, and I am unaccustomed to dealing with a gentleman in a high passion. You make me think it would have been wiser not to come here alone.'

'You fear me?' he asked incredulously. 'Oh, my dearest, I would not harm you ... But see ... I am cool again.' Releasing me, he stepped away. 'Let us walk.'

He tucked my hand beneath his arm, holding me close to his side as we walked away from the house and towards the surrounding wall.

'What are you thinking?' he asked suddenly.

'I was enjoying the night. The moors look mysterious with the moonlight moving over them, as though they were alive.'

'Many young women would be afraid.'

'I expect you know more about it than I do,' I replied lightly. 'I have seldom been out in the darkness with young women.'

'Or with men?'

I looked up at him resentfully. 'I am insulted, sir.'

'Forgive me. I am consumed by jealousy when I think ...'

'A governess has little opportunity for dalliance, even if she is so inclined,' I said.

'Which you are not?'

'I think you know I am not.'

'Then may I take it that I am being especially honoured by your company tonight?'

'You may.'

Piers stopped walking and turned to me. 'Georgiana. I must tell you. This is not an unusual occurrence for me. I have had many brief flirtations, so many that I am bitterly ashamed of myself. I never believed that I could feel as I feel now. I strayed where the fancy took me, without thought for the future. If only I had known that I would find you ... Can you forgive me?'

'It is no more than I had already guessed,' I replied. 'Young men are young men the world over, and must try their wings, I suppose. But please tell me no more about it.'

'There is little enough to tell. I remember none of them now, not since the day I saw you. I only know that before I was deceived by the sham and now I have found a real love.' He stroked my cheek gently, his face close to mine. 'That is what you have shown to me, Georgiana. You are my only love. From this day on. I swear it.'

His voice was solemn and sincere, but I still had doubts. Thus did men seduce unsuspecting women, with fair words and tender caresses.

He began to take me in his arms, then abruptly withdrew and stood holding me by the shoulders, looking deep into my eyes.

'One thing more, so that there shall be no more misunderstandings. The love that I have for you will accept no less than a display for all the world to see. Georgiana, I want you for my wife. It is the only way I shall be satisfied.'

I had hoped for it, prayed for it, but to hear the word spoken sent my head spinning. It *was* true. He had meant every word he had spoken to me.

'Answer me,' Piers ordered, almost shaking me. 'I told you to have your answer ready.'

'You did,' I said unsteadily, laughing a little. 'But you did not tell me what the question was to be.'

'You know it now,' he said, his voice low and fierce. 'Tell me, Georgiana. Will you marry me?'

'But your family . . .'

He threw his hands up in the air. 'Woman, you will send me mad! Forget my family. I shall deal with them if it becomes necessary. Do I have to beat you to make you answer?'

'You do not. I will marry you, Piers, if you really wish it.'

'Wish it? It is my dearest dream. Come here and let me show you how much I wish it.'

He clasped me to him, his lips finding mine, his arms pressing me close to his body. I had never been embraced in such a way and was half-frightened by the ferocity of it, bewildered by the feelings which swarmed up inside me and made me cling to him, returning his kisses with a fervour I had not suspected myself capable of. As his lips moved to my ear and my throat I opened my eyes, and saw something which brought me down with a jolt from the sweet heights.

Beyond Piers' shoulder, high on the ridge of the moors, was that strange horseman who had haunted me since I came to Delfdale.

'What is it?' Piers took one look at my face

and swung round, looking up to the black figure on the hilltop.

'Who is he?' I asked, clinging to his arm. 'Why does he sit there and watch the house, Piers? I have seen him before, the first night I was here, and Molly told me a strange tale of wolves and demons.'

Piers laughed and turned back to look at me. 'Molly is a woolly-head, my love. They call him the Wolf because it makes him seem eerie, and he has a pack of wolf-hounds which run with him and add to the legend. But in truth he is a harmless eccentric. He enjoys riding the moors at night, that is all.'

'But why does he come here?'

'Why not? No doubt he goes to other places, too.'

'But Molly said . . .'

'Molly, Molly.' Laughing, Piers kissed the end of my nose. 'Do not quote the servants at me, Georgiana. I know what they say. Most of it is sheer imagination. I have told you the truth. It may not be as exciting as the legend, but that is the way of life. The man is a lunatic.'

'You said he was a harmless eccentric.'

'I was being kind. In truth, I believe he is mad. From all accounts he leads a strange life, and what else can one think of a man who rides on the empty moors at night with huge dogs as companions?'

'He rides by daylight, too,' I said.

'So I believe. Many people claim to have seen him, but always at a distance. He shuns company. That is why people fear him and build tales around him. Forget him. He will not bother us. I doubt that he can even see us here in the shadows.'

The silhouette of the horseman remained outlined against the dark sky, appearing and disappearing as the moonshadows raced over him. Despite Piers' assurance, I was convinced that the Wolf was watching us. I could feel his hidden eyes on me, pricking my skin into a million tiny bumps.

Piers' arm came about my waist. 'Forget him,' he repeated.

'I can't. Please, Piers, let me go.' Pushing him away, I was suddenly aware of the chill of the night and shivered, drawing my cape more tightly around me.

'Frightened by a shadow?' he teased. 'Where's your mettle, my love? I tell you he cannot see us.'

'But I feel that he can. I am aware of him and cannot relax. What is he doing there, Piers?'

'Who can say? No-one that I know has ever met the man.'

'I have. At least, I almost met him.'

'You?' His voice was sharp. 'When?'

'On the day of Lucinda's accident. As I sat with her, a man appeared, riding a black stallion. He wore a hooded cloak, so I could not see his face, but he had a big grey dog with him.'

'How far away was he?'

'Not far. And he came closer, as close to me as we are to that wall. I spoke to him, Piers. I said something about Lucinda being hurt by a fall from her horse.'

'And what did he say?'

'Nothing. That was the strangest part. He was silent. But he is not dumb, for I heard him speak to the dog before he rode away. He had seen you coming.'

Piers was quiet for a long moment, his head bent so that I could not read his expression.

'If you had not returned at that moment,' I said, 'I think he might have spoken to me. Yet he did not seem inclined to help, as anyone else would have done. He was staring at me strangely.'

He glanced at me, frowning. 'You said he was hooded.'

'So he was. But I could feel his eyes on me, as I feel them now . . . Piers, I am not given to hysterical imaginings. He was there. If he shuns the society of other people, why did he approach so near to me?'

'I don't know. Who can guess the mind of a madman? But I am very glad that I did return in time. You might have been in danger.'

At that moment the hushing of the breeze was joined by another sound which tingled up and down my spine, the lonely, howling cry of a wolf-hound. Twice the noise reached out to surround us and then there was only the wind sighing across the empty land. When I looked up to the ridge, I saw that the Wolf had gone.

'It is late,' I said. 'I must go in, Piers.'

'You are cold, too. I can feel you shivering.' Placing an arm about my shoulders, he turned me back towards the house. 'We shall have no more clandestine meetings. In the morning I shall speak to my father about our marriage. There must be as little delay as possible.'

*　　*　　*

I slept little that night, my mind busy with thoughts of the past and of the future. I had always been certain that more lay in store than the life which others seemed to expect for me. That was why I rebelled against the cloistered life of the Rectory. I was not content to be quiet and demure, modest and subdued, as my sisters were, for I felt hemmed-in by the demands of convention.

My older sister, Christina, had accepted her lot and gone happily to marry a brown-faced, boorish farmer whom I despised. But mother and father seemed delighted by the match. For me they planned on a curate, or another farmer, or a merchant. They never looked above themselves and saw the chances for betterment, as I did.

I know that they despaired of me with my

undisciplined ways and sharp tongue. That was why they sent me away at the age of seventeen to stay with Colonel and Mrs Ford and their only daughter Louisa, in the hopes that the regimented household and the retiring girl would have some good effect on me. They did not. The tighter I was confined, the more I rebelled. I shocked poor Louisa with my outspoken views; appalled the Colonel by my love of wild riding; and caused Mrs Ford to have a fit of the vapours when I was discovered sharing a joke with the between-maid and a stable-lad. Back to the Rectory I went with despatch.

My parents, dear gentle souls that they were, decided that, since I would not be pleasant to the dull young men whom they invited to call, I might as well earn my living, as a governess. This profession, it was hoped, would impose some discipline on me and restrict my temptations. Perhaps it did, a little, or perhaps it was simply growing older which mellowed me, for it *was* only a mellowing. Nothing in the world could change my character completely.

I went to Arran Hall, to preside over the brood of Mr and Mrs Flaxon. The children, six of them, were a joy and their mother a great gossip. From her I learned of a great many things which my Rectory upbringing had hidden from me. I also learned about men, for Mr Flaxon had a variety of friends who stayed for short periods and seemed to think that the attempted seduction of the governess was part of the hospitality.

Eventually I told all to my friend Mrs Flaxon, who agreed that the situation was intolerable. She also told me, quite frankly, that she feared her own husband had designs on me, and so she thought it best for everyone that I should leave.

With Mrs Flaxon's help, I was brought to the attention of Lady Teignford, who engaged me to teach her son Alexander. In that household I saw more of the kind of life I dreamed was possible for myself, but again the only gentlemen to seek me out were those with the worst intentions so I began to despair of ever attaining the bright dream I held in my heart. When the dreadful Alexander finally brought about my dismissal, my hopes were at their lowest ebb. There seemed to be nothing left for me but to accept what fate had decreed from the beginning. I even despised myself for hoping for anything more.

And then Piers stepped in. Piers, who was all any woman could want in a man. I would be his wife and one day mistress of Moorhollow. My sons would be heir to the Cheviot fortune, my daughters able to enjoy the life which had escaped me as a child. So it was, after all, no sin to reach for the heights.

Among these happy thoughts, however, there kept intruding darker ones, doubtful ones. Lucinda, who vowed that she hated me, would not be pleased by the advancement of my position. I hoped that she had only spoken in a torment of fever, but I still shuddered when I remembered the glitter of hate in her eyes and the way she had forced her nails into my wrist.

There was Sophie, too, who despite our friendship enjoyed reminding me of my subservient position. That was something she could not do if I were betrothed to Piers.

Mr Cheviot might also be an obstacle. He approved of me as a companion to his wife, but would he accept me as happily as Piers' bride?

Of Annalie I had few doubts. The gentle girl would be pleased for me, I was sure.

But lastly, and oddest of all, for he had no real place in the pattern of my life, there was the Wolf. The thought of him roaming the moors with his dogs, isolated by his madness, disturbed me. For how many years would he continue to prowl the edges of our lives? I was curious about him, touched by compassion for the strange lonely life he led, so that thoughts of the Wolf, however irrational they might be, were inextricably mixed with the rest.

After church on that Sunday morning, Piers contrived to delay me long enough to murmur that he would be speaking to his father before luncheon and would come at once to tell me the result of the conversation. Therefore it was in a state of extreme nervousness that I joined Sophie and Annalie in the morning room, where Annalie inveigled me into giving her a lesson in French. Sophie interjected a phrase now and then, or corrected my pronunciation, but she soon tired of the game.

'Enough! I feel that I am in a school-room. And let us not forget that it is Sunday. We should rest, and think beautiful thoughts. Besides, Annalie, what good will it do you to learn to speak French? Are you proposing to travel abroad?'

Annalie looked at her hands and said dully, 'No.'

'Perhaps you have met an attractive Frenchman,' Sophie teased.

'I never meet anyone,' the girl replied, keeping her head lowered.

'If she wants to learn,' I said, 'there is no harm in it. We could all converse together.'

'To what purpose?' Sophie asked, her eyes bright and ingenuous. 'I have you to talk to, Georgie. I need no-one else . . . Oh, where are the men? What has Piers to say that is so urgent? Do you know?'

I hoped that Annalie would answer, but she was still apparently fascinated by the curling of her fingers.

Sophie gave her gurgling laugh. 'No reply? Ah, Georgie, shall I guess? Perhaps that blush on your cheek is my answer. Piers has talked much about you of late. What do you think,

Annalie?'

'I think,' the girl replied, standing up, 'I think that I shall go and visit Lucinda before lunch and see if there is anything she needs.'

'You are being very attentive to our invalid,' Sophie remarked.

Annalie glared at her sullenly. 'She is my sister. Do you wish me to ignore her?'

'No, indeed. Your loyalty is commendable.'

There was the faintest suggestion of sarcasm in the silky voice, bringing colour to Annalie's pale cheeks as she hurried from the room.

'Her conscience is still not easy,' Sophie said. 'And do not glare at me, Georgie. There is more on *your* mind than Annalie's tender feelings. Has Piers declared himself?'

The blunt question set me in a quandary. To a friend I might confess, but to Piers' step-mother . . .

Sophie smiled her knowing little smile. 'From your silence I would guess that he has. And being what you are, you would not settle for anything less than marriage. That is very wise of you.'

'Are you implying that I would marry Piers for his fortune?' I asked with resentment.

'It is a rôle forced upon women, unfortunately,' Sophie said, spreading her hands elegantly. 'But when the man is tall and handsome, too, we sometimes marry for love as well as security. My step-son is a most attractive man, is he not?'

'Yes, he is.'

'I knew you would have noticed. What woman would not? He has charm, looks, good manners, and the prospect of great wealth. In my opinion you are a fool to refuse him.'

'I did not ...' I began, and paused in confusion. Sophie's smile taunted me, obliging me to be frank with her. 'I have a feeling you knew the answer before you asked the question.'

'Ah, I cannot fool you, Georgie. You know me too well. Yes, I knew that Piers intended to propose to you. He told me so that I might prepare his father. Jonas was a little surprised by the swiftness of it, but I pointed out to him that our own courtship was very brief. I cannot conceive what is keeping them so long. The formal interview should have been over long ago ... But listen. They are coming. Now we shall know.'

Swift footsteps crossed the hall and the door opened to reveal a smiling Piers. He came to me, holding out his hands, and drew me from my seat.

'It is settled. You are to be my wife, Georgiana. From now on you are one of the family.' He pulled me to him, resting my head on his shoulder, and I closed my eyes against the tears of joy which pricked them.

Dreams, then, did sometimes come true. How sweet it was to be Georgiana Forrest on that day, and how easy these kind people had made it for me. Piers, Sophie, Mr Cheviot, Annalie, all were my good friends. And Lucinda I would bring round, given time, so that nothing could spoil my glorious future.

How naive I was, while thinking myself so worldly-wise. I had forgotten what my father always said, that human joy is never unalloyed by pain. Nor did I have the knowledge to guess the depths of wickedness to which people could sink. If I had not been so full of pride I might have known that my present happiness would have to be paid for later—with sorrow.

CHAPTER SIX

Life at Moorhollow became entirely different for me when I was wearing the sapphire ring which had belonged to Piers' mother. My room was no longer a lonely prison to which I retired when I was not wanted, but a place to sleep and be contented, for my days were filled with activity and companionship. I still spent a good deal of time with Sophie, but now that she was again assuming her normal life we were not confined to her boudoir, nor were we often alone. Piers would join us, and his father, and visitors came to the house to meet Piers' affianced bride. Instead of retiring from the scene on these occasions I was the centre of attraction.

I often found time to be with Annalie, continuing her lessons in French. She was not an apt pupil, but a hard-working one, and though our progress was slow it was steady. Our friendship grew, and although Annalie did not care to be too much in Sophie's company she seemed to enjoy being with me.

Piers and I were to be married in November. It would take some time to complete the arrangements and I had to have a new wardrobe of clothes, so there were many hours spent with the dressmaker, choosing patterns and materials, being measured and fitted. Sophie liked to supervise these sessions, though her taste was not mine and I flatly refused to be tricked out in too many frills and bows. On Sophie these looked well, for she was small and dainty, but on me they appeared grotesque and I preferred clean lines and plain colours.

Lucinda had not forgotten her animosity towards me, but she never spoke of it nor displayed it openly. When she was able to leave her bed and walk about with the aid of a crutch she often sat with us, though she had lost her old ebullience and had little interest in what was going on around her. She only came partially to life when her suitors came calling. They seemed to cheer her up by their presence, but once they were gone she reverted to her withdrawn silence and I guessed that she was worried about what might happen to her if she were permanently lamed. The doctor could not be sure until the leg was healed.

In the confidence of my elevated position in the family, I often took the opportunity for riding, either alone or with Piers. A more conventional household might have frowned on these activities, but at Moorhollow no-one raised an eyebrow. Alone with Smoke, the grey mare which had saved my life, I seldom strayed far from the house or the road, but when Piers came we would ride for miles across the moors, which he knew well.

The only thing which cast a slight shadow over my happy days was Piers' increasing boldness. I had to be careful when we were alone not to let him get too close, for his amorous advances gradually became more frequent and more demanding. It frightened and worried me, for I did not know exactly where the line lay which would prevent me from making myself a wanton or Piers from becoming an offended lover.

It was my habit to look from my window at night before going to bed, to watch the stars and the dark rise of the moors which I had come to love. Partly, too, I was looking for the Wolf. As the moon grew brighter again I expected every night to see the dark rider on the horizon. It was almost as if I knew that he would come again when there was light enough for him to see. And come he did.

I stood at my window in the darkened room, held fascinated by the sight of that motionless figure on the hilltop. Although he could not have seen me, I felt that it was at my window he stared. Such feelings were nonsense, of course, but they persisted and I knew I should never be completely at ease until I had discovered what brought the man to watch this house, for despite what Piers had said about him I remained convinced that the Wolf had some purpose in his visits to Moorhollow.

I had been standing there for several minutes, studying the outline of the man on the ridge in order that I might make a drawing of him later, when a soft noise made me turn in alarm. Instantly I was annoyed with myself for my nervousness. It was only someone tapping at my door. Dropping the curtain, I crossed the dark room.

'Piers!' Unconsciously my hand crept to the neckline of the light wrapper I wore over my nightgown, drawing it closer about my throat. The hour was late, close to midnight, and I could think of no reason, save one, for my future husband to come to my room at that time of night.

How handsome he was, his hair dishevelled, falling into blue eyes that burned me, his frilled shirt open at the neck revealing his strong throat.

'You should not have come,' I breathed. 'Suppose someone should see you?'

'They are all in bed,' he replied in a hoarse voice, and his hand came up to rest on the door, preventing me from closing it. 'Let me in, Georgiana.'

I began to protest, but had hardly opened my mouth before he applied his full strength to the door and pushed his way in, his arms curling about my waist and his mouth seeking mine. He was hot, his lips like fire against my skin and his hands feverishly searching for the belt of my wrapper even as he kicked the door closed. In the sudden darkness his breathing sounded loud and I fought his hands, repelled by the animal urgency I felt in him.

'Piers, no! Please don't! Piers!'

It was a nightmare. I tried to wrench away and succeeded only in tripping myself, so that I fell across the bed, wrapper and night gown ripping with a brief loud noise. I felt the night air cool on my naked breasts and Piers loomed above me, his shirt glowing palely in the thin strip of moonlight which came through the partly-open curtains.

Perhaps I should not fight, I thought. Perhaps this was what was expected of an engaged woman.

'Very well,' I said. 'If it must be, at least do not force me. It would be a pretty thing if you ravished your future wife.'

As I spoke, Piers fell to his knees and stayed there, bent low by the bed, groaning in some extremity I was too ignorant to understand. I lay staring at the dim ceiling, waiting for what was to come, and from outside there came the drawn-out, mournful cry of the Wolf's hounds. The sound made me shiver and draw my torn garments together.

'Georgiana.' Piers' voice, breathless but calm now, came out of the darkness as I sat up. He was sitting on the floor, looking up at me in the dimness. 'Forgive me, Georgiana. I must have been mad. Say that you forgive me.'

'Could you not have waited?' I asked, my voice tinged with the disgust I could not hide. 'Our wedding day is only eight weeks off.'

'To me it seems for ever.' He reached out and clutched my hand, pleading with me. 'Georgiana, please forgive me. I am a red-blooded man, and I love you beyond reason.'

'There was little of love in you tonight,' I said with a shudder. 'Love should be coloured with respect, with cherishing.'

He bent his head, laying it on my thigh. 'Don't be angry with me. Rather pity my weakness. Men are weak in these things. Didn't you know that?'

'I know that some men are, but when I have promised to marry you ... If you really love me you will be patient.'

'I will.' He pressed my hand to his lips. 'I promise you that I will.'

When he had gone I crept into bed and lay there staring at the ceiling with a feeling of sickness deep in my stomach. Was this, then, what a woman could expect from marriage? This uncaring roughness? I remembered my former employer Mrs Flaxon, who had told me that a woman must endure physical indignity for the sake of a name and security for herself and her children. And yet Sophie gloried in the secret side of marriage. Perhaps I would, too, when I had the confidence instilled by a wedding ring. But tonight ... I shivered. Tonight was an ugliness I preferred to forget.

*　　*　　*

I was almost afraid of meeting Piers again, but after that night he seemed a different man. Gentle, tender, most careful not to offend my modesty. In some ways I was pleased that we had at last reached a proper understanding of these matters, but I could not forget what he had done. My feelings towards him were undergoing a radical change.

*　　*　　*

Some days later, Sophie and I sat in the solarium enjoying the warmth of the autumn sun as it poured in through the glass dome. The room was crowded with plants in stone tubs, reminding me of nothing so much as the tropical house at Kew, where I had taken Alexander one day. It had not been a successful outing, for the boy had picked a rare bloom and we had been asked to leave.

The year was turning towards the end of September and Sophie's condition was beginning to show. She camouflaged it with loose wrappers, all frills and furbelows, which framed her lovely head and throat, but the pregnancy only served to improve her looks. Her hair shone, her skin was creamy, and her dark eyes had an added lustre.

We sat in companionable silence, Sophie reading a French novel by a person named George Sand, whom she assured me was female. I was busy with paper and pencils sketching at a small table. A drawing of Sophie had pleased her vanity, but now I was engaged on a depiction of the Wolf as I had seen him those few nights ago.

So engrossed in my task was I that I did not hear the door open and was surprised when Annalie spoke from behind me.

'I've been looking for you, Georgiana. Will you come with me to visit Miss Barber this afternoon? I hear she has been taken ill, poor soul, and . . .'

She stopped abruptly, staring at the paper on which I had been working.

'Why that's . . . Have you seen him, too?'

'He was there the other night,' I said.

'Yes, I know. He . . . He . . .' She paused in confusion, her cheeks filled with unnatural colour.

'Who are you talking about?' Sophie

85

demanded.

'The Wolf,' I told her.

She sighed and closed her book. 'If you are so bored, do please invent something pleasant.'

'It's no invention,' Annalie said stubbornly. 'The Wolf is real. Georgiana and I have both seen him. Look at this picture.'

For a few moments there was silence as Sophie perused my sketch. I had depicted the shape of man and horse in outline, with a cloak blowing from the man's shoulders.

'So this is he,' Sophie said eventually. 'You have made him look romantic, Georgie. I understood that he was a madman.'

I heard Annalie take a sharp breath as though she would deny this last, but she said nothing, merely glared at Sophie mutinously.

Sophie stood up, rearranging her flowing wrapper. 'I shall leave you to your fantasies. I do agree that there is very little excitement here at Moorhollow, but be careful not to believe too much of what you imagine.' With a shake of her head and a little, pitying smile, she left us, trailing a cloud of heady perfume in her wake.

'He is not mad!' Annalie said. 'Just because he likes to be out on the moors at night . . . He is probably a lonely man.'

'You think so?' I queried.

'I do. He keeps to himself, that is all. That is why people tell malicious lies about him.'

She was really angry in her defence of the Wolf and it puzzled me.

'What do you know of him?' I asked.

Annalie flushed, lowering her eyes. 'Very little. But I have seen him as I drive to and from the village. I think . . . I think he waits to see me, Georgiana. And at night he watches my window. If he were not so shy he might come and speak to me.'

'Annalie! Are you sure?'

'Not sure, but it is a more likely explanation than madness.'

Even so, it was a highly imaginative theory. But the Wolf did watch the house, from the side where Annalie's room lay directly below mine.

'How long has this been going on?' I asked.

Annalie considered, a frown appearing above her spectacles. 'About a year. Yes, it was last autumn when he first came. No-one had seen him before then, but he began to ride in this direction and the rumours came out of nowhere. Nobody really knows anything about him, but they fear him because of the way he dresses and the way he avoids any meeting, and those . . . those dogs. It is unjust. I believe he is simply a lonely young man.'

'Young?' I repeated. 'And handsome, too, I suppose?'

'I have never seen his face. But, yes, I believe he is a handsome man.'

Poor Annalie, I thought worriedly. Having

87

little hope of real romance she had built the mysterious figure of the Wolf into a fairy-tale prince. It was a dangerous thing to do.

'It was not wise to assume too much,' I said gently. 'You are unlikely to meet him, and you could be wrong. Perhaps the rumours were begun by someone who knows more of him than you do.'

Her lips set into stubborn lines. 'I still do not believe that he is mad. One day he will find the courage to approach me.'

I fervently hoped that nothing of the sort would occur. The Wolf boded no good for any of us. I should know. Apparently I had come closest of anyone to a meeting with him, and I still remembered the fear I had felt on that occasion.

Unfortunately, neither Annalie nor myself could guess how soon her romantic dream was to be shattered.

*   *   *

Annalie and I drove to the village in the pony-trap and found Miss Barber ill in bed. Her companion, Miss Luce, was distraught with worry. She was convinced that Miss Barber was at death's door, but, having seen the lady, I myself thought that she was exaggerating her illness in order to gain attention.

'I don't know what I shall do without her,' Miss Luce wailed as we sipped tea. The tears rolled freely down her lined face and her whole tiny body expressed misery in every line. 'We have been together for nearly thirty years. And she has been my only friend. If anything should happen to her . . .'

'Did not the doctor say that she needed only to rest?' Annalie said gently. 'I'm sure you need not worry, Miss Luce. Georgiana and I are sure that Miss Barber will recover very soon. Make sure she has the calves' foot jelly that we brought. It will give her strength.'

'Oh, I will. I will.' The old lady smiled through her tears. 'You are so kind, Annalie. And you, too, Miss Forrest. I assure you that I shall do everything in my power to nurse my dear friend back to health and strength. It would be too awful if we lost her. I declare I simply do not know what I should do if I were left alone in the world.'

Her monologue of distress was interrupted by the arrival of the curate, a large, fresh-faced young man named Roger Sims. As he greeted us all I could not help but notice how his expression changed when he looked at Annalie. He was told that Miss Barber was resting but might see him shortly, and then there came a summons for Miss Luce to attend the invalid.

As the old lady left her chair she swayed momentarily and the curate took her arm, but she protested that she was quite all right.

'It appears to me,' I said when the door was

closed, 'that Miss Luce is the more ill of the two. It cannot be good for her chasing up and down stairs all day.'

'But Georgiana . . .' Annalie began, caught Mr Sims' eye on her and flushed into silence.

'Miss Barber is ill, is she not?' the curate said.

'I don't doubt that she feels unwell,' I replied, 'but that is no reason for her to pretend she is dying and insist on attention the whole time.'

'You know something of doctoring?' Mr Sims said sceptically.

'A little, and quite an amount about people. I have every sympathy for Miss Barber, but even more for Miss Luce.'

As usual, I was speaking my mind when I should not, and Annalie decided that she must excuse my behaviour. She looked up at the curate, scarlet-faced.

'Miss Forrest is always f-f-frank,' she got out. 'But she is not unkind. P-Perhaps she is right. Miss Luce d-did look ill.'

'I shall be pleased to see what I can do about it,' Mr Sims said softly. 'Miss Barber would be lost without Miss Luce. Perhaps, if I think you are correct, I might gently remind her that Miss Luce is not as young as she was.'

'Thank you,' Annalie said, and lowered her eyes to the teacup in her lap.

'Not at all,' he replied. 'I know how fond of them both you are, Miss Annalie. If I can do

90

anything to prevent you distress . . . anything at all . . .'

Very shortly after this, Annalie and I left the house and returned to the pony and trap.

'You have an admirer, I see,' I remarked as I took the reins and urged the pony to a trot.

'I have?' Annalie looked bewildered. 'Who?'

'Mr Sims, of course. If you had not kept your eyes so firmly on the floor you would have seen the way he looked at you.'

'He is just being kind,' she said dully. 'He sees how dreadfully nervous I am and wants to soothe me. It is his Christian duty.'

'Perhaps. But I am sure there is more to it. Behind the clerical garb there is a man like any other, with thoughts and feelings that have nothing to do with his calling.'

Annalie looked at me hopefully. 'Do you really think so?'

'I do. The next time he calls at Moorhollow you must look and see for yourself. It will be more productive than building dreams around someone whose face you have never seen.'

'But Mr Sims will never dare speak to me, even if you are right. He is not a rich man. Lucinda's beaus . . .'

'From what I have seen of them,' I replied crisply, 'none of them have the qualities Mr Sims possesses. Kindness. Gentleness.'

'Would you swap Piers for Mr Sims?' Annalie asked.

'Indeed not!' I said with a laugh. 'I should not make a good wife for any churchman. I am much too uncontrolled.'

We passed through the village, crossed the bridge beside the church, and began to climb the tree-lined road towards the valley end. The leaves were changing colour, some of them drifting down across our path, and I was feeling in the best of spirits until a horseman stepped from the trees ahead of us.

There was no mistaking the black-clothed figure of the Wolf.

Reining in the pony, I glanced at Annalie. She was sitting tensely, her hands clasping her reticule, but she seemed unafraid.

The Wolf urged the stallion forward and grasped the pony's bridle, staring at me from the folds of the hood. I saw a pair of burning black eyes, and I was afraid, as I had been before. He was a big man. Malignancy radiated from him, paralysing my vocal chords.

'They say you are going to marry Piers Cheviot. Is it true?' His voice was deep, harsh with suppressed anger.

'What is it to you?' I asked hoarsely. 'Is this the way a gentleman behaves? Unhand the pony, sir, and clear the way.'

'I am no gentleman,' he said. 'Answer me!'

Annalie clutched at my arm, saying in a small voice, 'It's true. But do not be so rough with us. We want to be your friends.'

'Friends.' He repeated the word with grim

amusement. 'I have no friends, Miss Cheviot, nor do I wish for any, especially if they are related to Piers Cheviot. You may give him a message for me. Tell him it is an eye for an eye, and a tooth for a tooth ... Step down from the trap, Miss Forrest.'

I stared at him in stupefaction. What did he intend to do?

'I said step down!' he ordered furiously. 'Or do I have to make you?'

As he began to move the stallion forward his hand left the bridle. I seized the chance, slapped the reins and shouted at the pony. The stallion wheeled away and we were past. But not for long. I was aware of the horse drawing level with us, the man reaching out. A strong arm locked about my waist and lifted me. The reins dragged at my hands. I saw the pony turn aside with the pressure. Then I had to let go.

Suddenly I was dropped. I hit the ground awkwardly and fell in a heap. By the time I had struggled up, the Wolf had leapt from his saddle. Behind him I saw the trap had come to a halt across the road and Annalie was sitting with her hands to her face, a wordless moan coming from her mouth.

The Wolf grabbed me by the shoulder, pulling me round to face him.

'So,' he said. 'Piers Cheviot's woman has spirit, has she?'

I lifted my head high and looked him in his shadowed eyes. 'Spirit enough!' I said breathlessly. 'I am not afraid of *you*. If you touch me, Piers will kill you.'

'Let him try.' With a brusque motion of his hand he threw back the hood and stood bareheaded, glaring at me. His hair was dark, but beyond that I saw nothing but a fierce scar slashing across the left side of his face from chin to temple. It held my gaze, horrifying me as I imagined the kind of wound it must have been.

'Handsome, am I not?' he said sardonically. 'Why don't you faint, or show some maidenly revulsion?'

'Is that what you expect?'

'I expect nothing. But I wanted you to see this. I have Piers Cheviot to thank for it.'

'If Piers did that then you must have deserved it.'

'Indeed,' he said flatly. 'You think so.'

'Is this why you accosted us?' I demanded, finding my temper. 'Annalie has been frightened out of her wits because of this? You are a devil, sir, preying on helpless women in this way. Have you not the courage to face Piers man to man?'

'Aye, I have the courage for that. But it is not what I want. Death is too good for him, too swift and merciful.' He reached out and took me by the shoulders, his fingers bruising me. 'We shall meet each other again one day, he and I, but it will be at a time of my own choosing, after I have done to him what he did

94

to me.'

One hand came under my chin, pulling my face upwards, and he bent swiftly, forcing his lips onto mine with harsh brutality. His hands held my arms, preventing me from fighting, though I struggled fiercely against that ghastly embrace. Then suddenly I was free, gasping and scrubbing my hand across my mouth.

The Wolf had turned away and swung easily to the stallion's back, from where he addressed me grimly.

'A sample only. Take heed of it. Don't marry Piers Cheviot. Leave this place. I shall know if you remain, and you can expect to see me again, at any hour, day or night. Nor will you escape so lightly the next time. Remember that.'

He dug his heels into the stallion's flanks and rode into the trees, up the hill, and as he disappeared from sight Annalie jumped from the trap and came to fling herself into my arms.

'Georgiana! Georgiana!' she wept. 'Oh, that dreadful man! That wicked, sinful man. How wrong I was. How foolish!'

I patted her shoulder, feeling strangely calm. At least now I knew why the Wolf haunted Moorhollow.

'You were not entirely wrong,' I said. 'He is young.'

She looked up at me, shuddering. 'But his face ... Oh, they are right about him,

Georgiana. He is mad. Raving mad!'

I did not agree, but I did not tell her so. She was trembling and weeping and my main concern was to get her home.

In my own mind I was quite sure that the Wolf was as sane as myself. He had behaved badly—wickedly, even—but it was not madness that caused it. It was intense, deadly fury.

CHAPTER SEVEN

Annalie, it transpired, had not heard my conversation with the Wolf. Even so, she had heard and seen enough to tell a story that shocked her family.

'It's an outrage!' Mr Cheviot blustered. 'An outrage! The man should be locked up. Where does he live?'

Silence greeted this question, then Annalie spoke up.

'No-one knows, Papa. They say he lives in a castle, on a cliff. But no-one knows where it is.'

Her father turned his small eyes on her and his lip curled. 'A castle? Oh, come, my dear. Surely even you do not believe such arrant nonsense. Where do you hear these tales?'

'The servants make them up,' Sophie's voice, soft and sulky, joined in the conversation. 'Clearly the man is deranged.

These threats against Piers ...' Her eyes turned languidly to her step-son. 'Have you done anything against this man, Piers?'

'I have never even met him,' Piers replied heatedly. 'Naturally I've heard the rumours and seen him prowling the moors, but what he imagines I have done to him ... All the same, if I see him again I shall make sure I meet him. There's a score I have to settle with him now.' He glanced at me protectively, reaching out to take my hand in a clasp of reassurance.

Mr Cheviot strode ponderously across the room and returned to his stance by the fireplace.

'I shall endeavour to discover the whereabouts of this man. Someone must know where he lives. What is his real name?'

This time there was no reply.

'I see.' Mr Cheviot chewed his lip. 'Very well, leave the matter in my hands. Piers—I want no heroics. If the man ...'

'Heroics?' Piers came to his feet, hands clenched. 'After what he did to Georgiana ... you expect me to let him get away with it?'

'No. I simply tell you that you will control yourself. Your anger does you credit, my boy, but if the man is not sane you will be running an unnecessary risk. Georgiana was not really harmed, and no-one else will ever hear of it ... No, Piers, you will do as you are told until I discover the truth of this matter.'

As I was going down to dinner that evening

I encountered Piers on the stairs, where he had apparently been waiting for me.

'Are you feeling quite well?' he asked anxiously. 'After that unpleasant experience . . .'

'I feel very well,' I assured him. 'But I must talk with you, Piers.'

'And I with you. Meet me in the library after dinner.'

In the drawing-room later, Lucinda played the piano and sang, mainly for the benefit of the young man who had been invited to spend the evening with us. He was the son of gentry who lived some distance from Moorhollow and it was apparent that he enjoyed Mr Cheviot's full approval.

Lucinda looked particularly lovely that night in a blue gown which brought out the colour of her eyes, her golden hair piled high and a diamond pendant at her throat. For some time now I had felt that her animosity towards me was waning as her strength returned. We were not friends, but neither were we open enemies. Most of the time she avoided or ignored me.

Tonight, however, it was apparent that she was aware of no-one beside Garnet Phelps. He leaned on the piano, gazing down into her eyes, while she smiled at him coquettishly and sang love songs.

Piers had not joined us after dinner, so I assumed he had gone straight to the library. Soon I made excuses and went to meet him.

But Piers was not in the library. The fire was dying there and I had to light the lamp. Choosing a book, I sat down to read it, while the grandfather clock in the corner ticked loudly through the silence.

Suddenly a sound made the hairs on my neck rise with horror. It was the sound I had heard before, the howling of the great dogs who accompanied the Wolf. He was out there somewhere, watching and waiting.

Turning the lamp down to a tiny glimmer, I went to the window and slipped behind the curtains. Gradually, I made out the shape of the trees bending with the wind. The moon was just rising above the ridge, full and white in cold majesty.

The dog howled again, but I could not see it, nor any sign of its master.

Then I froze. The door of the library had creaked and someone had come in. I remained statue-like behind the curtain, my heart thumping.

'Georgiana?'

'Piers!' Thankfully, I came out of my hiding-place. 'Oh, you gave me a fright!'

'What are you doing behind the curtain?' he asked as I turned up the lamp.

'I heard a dog howling. The Wolf is out there, Piers. He told me he would be nearby, watching to see whether I stayed or went away.'

'You said nothing of this when we spoke to

my father.'

'No. I felt I must talk to you alone first.'

'I see.' His expression was grave. 'What else did he say to you, Georgiana?'

'Does it matter? If you have never met him, then nothing he said can be true.'

'Tell me anyway. At least let me know what is in my enemy's mind.'

I sank down into a chair, wondering, wondering. If the Wolf was mad, what did it matter what he said?

'He has a scar on his face,' I told Piers, tracing a line from my eye corner to my chin. 'He said that you caused it and he would not rest until he had done the same to you. And he told me that if I did not leave he would come again for me.'

'Why?' Piers asked with a frown. 'Why you? Did he not tell you why you were included in all this?'

'I would have thought his reasons were plain. If I were frightened enough, you might seek him out. And that would save him the trouble of approaching you. He has been waiting for nearly a year, I understand.'

His face sharpened. 'He told you that?'

'Annalie said it is almost a year since he first began to be seen on the moor. Where does he come from, Piers?'

'Bedlam, for all I know. I tell you, Georgiana, the man is crazy. I swear to you—if he has a scar on his face it was not I who caused it.'

It sounded like the truth.

'I have made a decision,' he went on firmly, thrusting his hands into his pockets. 'You must leave Moorhollow until this business is settled.'

'Leave?' I stared at him in astonishment. 'I shall do nothing of the kind. I am not afraid.'

'But I am.' He was beside me in one stride, kneeling by the chair and lifting my hand to his cheek. 'As long as you stay here you are in danger. I can't risk that. You must go to your sister. When it is safe, I shall come for you.'

'No, Piers. You once told me that you had not fallen in love with a helpless, fainting female. I have not changed. The Wolf will not dare to come into the house, and I shall not go out without protection. I do not intend to run away. My place is to be at your side. You're the one who is threatened, not I.'

'But you *must* go!' he said passionately. 'You must!'

'I think not. I shall stay, and we shall be married as we planned. Let the Wolf do his worst. He will see that he cannot intimidate us.'

Piers buried his face in my skirts, his hand holding mine so tightly that the knuckles were white. Looking down at his bent head, I stroked his hair consolingly, and wondered at the truth of all this. The Wolf was no madman, except perhaps in his lust for revenge. Yet why

101

should Piers lie to me?

*   *   *

'So your Wolf provided a little diversion,' Sophie remarked as we sat by the fire the next day, she doing nothing while Annalie embroidered a silk cushion for the baby and I crocheted a shawl. Lucinda was there, too, sitting apart from us, dreaming at the piano.

'You will agree,' I replied with a smile, 'that life here is not quite so uneventful as you thought.'

Sophie surveyed me thoughtfully, her dark eyes opaque. 'It seems to amuse you. Piers is extremely worried. I gather he asked you to go away from here for a while.'

'Yes, he did. But I should think poorly of myself if I let the Wolf frighten me into running away.'

'Besides,' Annalie put in, 'the threats were against Piers, not Georgiana.'

'Ah—yes.' Sophie was still watching me narrowly. 'You have courage, Georgie. I confess that if it had happened to me I should have left just as fast as I could.'

There was a stir of skirts behind us and Lucinda said flatly, 'Surely no-one expects Georgiana to leave now? Why, the wedding is to be held in a few weeks time . . . I want to go down to the stables. Will someone come with me?'

102

'I will,' Annalie said at once.

'Oh, not you!' Lucinda's voice was scornful. 'What do you know of horses? Merely to look at one frightens you.'

Annalie bent her head to hide the flush of hurt that stained her cheeks.

'You do not expect me to go, I hope?' Sophie said patting her stomach. 'The air is chill this morning, and the smell of the stables, *ach*, it would upset *bébé*.'

'Of course,' Lucinda said with the faintest hint of derision, 'you must take care of yourself.'

I looked round at her, saying, 'I should be pleased to come with you, if you would care for my company.' Here, at last, was a chance to talk with Lucinda, perhaps to make friends with her.

'I would,' Lucinda said. 'You, at least, share my love of horses.'

The day was cool and a mist lay across the valley. Lucinda and I made our way to the stables, she depending heavily on her crutch, though she refused any help from me.

The stable-lad touched his cap and opened the door for us.

'Morning, Miss Cheviot.'

Lucinda inclined her head coolly. 'Good morning, Fred. Miss Forrest and I have come to look at the horses. How is Velvet today?'

'A bit fretful, miss,' the lad replied, following us into the gloomy stable where the aromatic

103

tang of horses and straw closed round us. 'I think she might need a bit of exercise, with your permission, miss. A bit more than she's getting, that is. A good run would do her the world of good.'

Lucinda had moved to the stall where Velvet stood and was offering sugar, stroking the mare's glossy head. In the adjoining stall the grey mare which was my usual mount shifted restlessly.

'You may be right,' Lucinda said. 'She's been used to a good deal of exercise. Georgiana, would you care to take her out?'

'I should love it,' I replied with enthusiasm, 'if someone is free to accompany me.'

'Why not alone?' Lucinda asked. 'You often ride out alone. Are you afraid of the moor?'

'No, but there is a mist today, and after what happened yesterday . . .'

'Oh, come!' she exclaimed, her face suddenly hard. 'You carry the game too far.'

'Game?'

'This nonsense of the Wolf.' Her eyes flashed scorn at me. If she had been able to, she would have stamped her foot. 'It was imaginative of you to have Annalie as a witness. Her distress blinded everyone to your own calmness. *You* were the one who should have been upset—*if* it had been true.'

'It *was* true,' I said in a low voice. 'It happened as we told it.'

'I don't doubt it. But what did he say to you

when Annalie could not hear? . . . No, do not answer. You would only lie. But I am not so stupid, Miss Forrest. I know exactly what it is all about.'

Eyes starting from his head, the stable-lad was an avid listener to this exchange. Soon all the servants would hear of it.

'I shall be interested to hear your theory,' I said, 'but let us discuss it elsewhere.'

'No!' She tossed her head proudly and lifted a stubborn chin. 'We shall talk here. No-one is likely to come to your rescue. Oh, you may walk away. You can go more swiftly than I. But if you do I shall go straight to Papa and tell him what I know. He will listen to *me*.'

'Very well. But at least let us be alone.' I flung a meaningful glance at Fred, who swiftly withdrew. But I knew he would not be far away.

'Do you realize the servants will all hear of this?' I said in a low voice.

'Servants? Why should I care, when what I say is the truth? They may as well learn what you are now, as later.'

'And what am I?' I asked angrily.

'A fortune-hunter! . . . Oh, yes, Miss Forrest. When the engagement was announced I knew that it was what you had planned all the time. I had suspected something from the beginning. You are not the type to be a companion—not for long.'

'Lucinda . . .'

'Be quiet!' She was leaning against a beam and now brought up her crutch, placing the end between the slots of the stall so that I was imprisoned in a corner. 'I will listen to no more lies ... You have everyone else in your power. Sophie is so stupid and selfish she thinks of nothing but her own comfort. That is how you came to be employed, no doubt. Papa would agree to anything to please her. He is besotted. And you soon had Piers blinded by passion for you, and Annalie following at your heels. She will like anyone who is kind to her. But all the time I have been watching you and puzzling about your real intentions. I thought you were only after Piers' inheritance, but now I see there is much more to it than that. Much, much more. It is a plot—between you and your paramour.'

My astonishment turned to bewilderment. Paramour? What wild theory had Lucinda formulated?

'I can conceive of nothing that could have given you such an idea,' I said, truly perplexed.

'Can you not?' Her eyes shone with triumph and I saw the tip of her tongue run round her lips. 'Then I shall tell you. You see, Miss Forrest, I have guessed your strategem. You will marry Piers and give him an heir. And then he will be killed—by the Wolf, of course. But no-one will ever find the Wolf. He does not exist, except in legend. It was your lover who accosted you yesterday. A ploy to make everyone believe in the Wolf ... And when Piers is dead, leaving you the mother of the young heir, you will remarry—after a suitable time, no doubt—and bring your lover to act as Prince consort.'

I stared at her in disbelief. 'There is neither logic nor sense in what you are saying. Do you really hate me enough to believe this rigmarole? What of the horseman who has been seen on the moors for this past year, long before I came?'

'I have never seen him,' she said haughtily.

'Annalie has—and so have the servants. Molly told me ...'

'Molly! She has less wits than a sheep. Maybe once something strange was seen. From that the legend has grown. As for Annalie—she will believe anything. She lives in a world of make-believe.'

I felt suddenly sorry for her. 'What a lonely person you must be, Lucinda. Do you care for no-one?'

'I care for my family,' she raged. 'I care about Moorhollow. My father has worked all his life for what he has and it belongs to us—to the Cheviots—not a governess with ideas above her station.' Her breast heaved as she paused for breath.

'One thing you appear to have ignored,' I said. 'Suppose Sophie's baby should be a boy? That would ruin what you seem to think is my plan, for in the event of Piers' death the child would become your father's heir.'

Lucinda frowned, staring at me unblinkingly, but after a moment she had found her answer. 'A baby is easy to dispose of. A pillow on his face; a window left open in winter . . . And who is to say that it will live? Sophie is not strong. Perhaps she and her baby will both die.'

I took hold of the crutch which barred my way. 'Let me go, Lucinda. I will listen to no more of these ravings. It is clear to me that the fever affected your mind. You are accusing me of planning murder!'

'Yes.' She was pressing the crutch into place with her full weight. 'Murder and worse than murder. But one thing I promise you, Miss Forrest. You will never marry my brother. If you do not leave Moorhollow you will be sorry.'

Using all my strength, I pushed the crutch out from the slots. The movement caught Lucinda off balance. She toppled. I reached out and caught her in my arms, propelling her to where she could hold onto an upright beam, while the grey mare, restless already, began to rear and whinny, disturbed by the commotion.

'I should have let you fall!' I said angrily.

'Perhaps you should, Miss Forrest.' Her face was close to mine and I saw the cold hatred in her eyes. 'Perhaps you should. No matter what you do, it will not make me change my mind. I know there is some plot afoot, even if I have

108

got the details wrong, and I warn you that I shall do everything in my power to stop you . . . My stick, if you please!'

For too long I had been used to obeying orders. The crutch lay on the straw-scattered floor. I bent obediently to pick it up, and looked round in time to see a heavy lantern swinging straight for my head.

* * *

I awoke in my own bed, with Piers, Annalie and a doctor in attendance. My head was heavily bandaged and hurting so much that I could hardly bear to open my eyes.

'You must rest,' the doctor said. 'Stay in bed for a few days. I'll order a light diet for you. And in future be a little more careful of approaching horses in their stalls.'

He closed his bag and left us. I saw that Annalie had been weeping.

'We have all been so worried, my love,' Piers told me, pressing my hand. 'Thank heaven you will recover. I would not have believed that Smoke was so vicious if I had not seen the evidence for myself, but she has been less controllable than any mare we have ever had.'

'But Piers . . . I don't understand,' I breathed. 'The grey mare . . .'

'She does not remember what happened,' Annalie guessed, one hand on her brother's shoulder as she looked down at me woefully.

'You remember going to the stable with Lucinda?' Piers asked me. 'The grey was restless.'

'Yes.'

'You were concerned. I know you have been fond of the animal ever since you encountered her. You were opening the door of the stall when Lucinda stumbled and would have fallen had you not caught her. Her crutch fell into the stall. When you bent to pick it up, the mare lashed out and kicked you.'

Even in my dazed condition I knew it was not the mare who had injured me. I clearly remembered every word and every event. So Lucinda had made up the story. It would be her word against mine.

'You were still lying there when I came,' Piers continued. 'Lucinda managed to pick up the stick and came out to the yard just as I was arriving home. She was almost incoherent with shock, and so was I when I saw you on the floor of that stall, in danger of being trampled to death. I shall go at once and put a bullet through that damned horse.'

'No! No, don't do that. The mare is not vicious. Please, Piers.'

His face twisted. 'Very well. She shall have a second chance. But at the least sign of another attack I shall personally take a pistol to her . . . Now you must rest.'

* * *

For several days I was confined to my bed, unable to move without being assailed by sickness and dizziness. During this time, I told no-one of what had really happened in the stable. It was a matter between Lucinda and myself.

*   *   *

'You still look pale, poor Georgie,' Sophie sympathized when she came to see me one evening. 'Annalie tells me you intend to come down tomorrow. Is that wise?'

'I can't lie here for ever,' I said.

'But a few more days would not hurt. Be sure you are strong enough, chérie. You want to be really well for your wedding, do you not?'

'Of course I do. I shall take it slowly, I promise.'

'Good.' She patted my hand. 'We all miss you, Georgie. And Lucinda, especially, will be pleased to see you among us again. She is still in a shocked state. She has not been near the stable since you were hurt. It seems that she has forgotten her passion for horses.'

'Temporarily, I'm sure,' I said. It was not surprising that Lucinda avoided the stable which held memories of her own violence.

'Has she been to see you?' Sophie asked.

'I did not expect her. She has difficulty in climbing stairs, and I doubt that we should

111

know what to say to each other.'

Sophie smiled her mischievous, conspiratorial smile. 'Unlike you and I, eh, Georgie? We have been good friends, have we not?'

'I hope we always shall be,' I replied, though I was puzzled by her references to Lucinda. It was almost as though she knew that there was more to my 'accident' than appeared on the surface.

*   *   *

Completely rested by my stay in bed, I rose early the next morning. I was brushing out my hair when a piercing scream rang through the house, followed by a woman's voice shouting incoherently.

As I ran to see what was happening, I realized that the voice belonged to Sophie's maid, Babette.

On the first floor I encountered Piers and Annalie, who were both hurrying towards the main bedrooms, from where the noise emanated. Piers was in his shirtsleeves and Annalie dressed in a nightgown and wrapper, her hair still in its night-time pig-tail.

'*Madame! Madame!*' Babette wailed. '*Oh, ce n'est pas vrais! Éveillez-vous!*'

'Stop that noise!' Mr Cheviot's voice, louder than I had ever heard it, cut short the Frenchwoman's lamentation just as we reached the open door of Sophie's room.

Babette knelt by one side of the bed, her hands clasped in an attitude of prayer, while great tears coursed down her thin face. On the opposite side of the bed Mr Cheviot bent. I could see that he was holding Sophie's hand, though his body hid her face.

'Is she ill?' Piers demanded.

'*Elle est morte!*' Babette wept. '*Madame est morte!*'

Dead? It was not possible. I remember feeling stunned, then Annalie gasped and swayed towards me, so that I had to put my arm around her. She was trembling violently.

Mr Cheviot looked round, the veins on his face standing out in fine red tracery against a sickly yellow background.

'Fetch a doctor,' he said. 'Fetch Georgiana.'

'It's too late for that,' Piers said roughly. 'My God, look at her! How did this happen? She's been . . .'

Babette began to wail again, her head in her hands, and as Mr Cheviot looked up at his son I saw Sophie's face. It was swollen, blue-tinged . . .

A little scream came from Annalie's throat and she pressed her face into my shoulder, sobbing. As I tried to comfort her I saw that Lucinda had come to the door and was staring at me.

'Been what?' she asked. 'What's happened to Sophie?'

'You ladies get away from here,' Piers ordered. 'Georgiana, send someone for the doctor. He can't help her now, but he can at least verify the cause of . . .'

'Piers!' His father called his attention from us. 'Look at this. She had it in her hand, clutching it.'

As it passed from one to the other I saw that the object was a piece of black cloth with silver braid attached. Piers frowned over it and showed it to Babette, who denied that she had ever seen it before.

'Let me see,' Lucinda said, and Piers brought the item to the door, holding it on the palm of his hand.

The sight of it was a further shock, for I recognized that piece of frogging.

'Nobody here has anything like that,' Lucinda said in a hushed voice. 'She must have torn it off . . .'

Piers was watching me, had noted the look on my face.

'Georgiana?'

'It looks like . . .' I began.

'It was the Wolf!' Annalie said hysterically. 'He was wearing that coat when he stopped us. The Wolf . . . The Wolf murdered Sophie!'

CHAPTER EIGHT

Annalie lay on a chaise longue in the drawing-room, clasping a bottle of smelling salts and a wet handkerchief, while Lucinda and I sat on opposite sides of the fire occupied by our own thoughts.

The local constable had arrived in his blue serge uniform with the brass buttons down the front and was being shown the scene of the crime by Piers, while Mr Cheviot was closeted in the library with Roger Sims. We all knew now that Sophie had been brutally murdered, suffocated with one of her own pillows. It was a double murder, for the baby, too, had died. It was not a pleasant thing to contemplate.

Had I been wrong about the Wolf? I wondered. He would have to be insane to do this dreadful thing to Sophie. His quarrel was with Piers. But if he had wanted to kill he had had both Annalie and myself at his mercy only a week ago. Why risk an entry into the house? Madmen were said to be fiendishly cunning.

Somewhere in the back of my mind, suffocation raised an echo of memory. A pillow. Who had said that? A pillow on the face . . . Of course! Lucinda had said that was how I might plan to murder the child. Had she done this to throw suspicion on me, through the person she so firmly believed was my accomplice—the Wolf?

Startled by the thought, I looked across and found Lucinda watching me closely, her eyes bright with loathing. When I met her gaze she said thickly, 'That is one of your problems solved, anyway. Sophie will never produce another heir now.'

The malevolence of her tone appalled me.

'This is not the time to revive those stupid accusations,' I said fiercely, glancing at Annalie, who appeared to be asleep.

'No? Why not? They are looking for the culprit. You can tell them where he can be found. I think I shall call the constable.'

'Yes, do.' I was angry, tired of her twisted imaginings, and my head ached, the pain stemming from the half-healed wound where the lantern had caught me. 'Fetch him. And while he's here I shall tell him what really happened in the stable.'

Lucinda blanched. 'He won't believe you. No-one will. Not now.'

'Nor will anyone believe you, if you air your jealous lies. I know nothing about the Wolf.'

'So you say. But how did he get into the house unless someone let him in? How did he know the way to Sophie's room? And why did he kill the one person who stood in your way?'

'Sophie was my friend!' I said in a choked voice.

'Friend? She hated you. She knew what you were plotting. We talked about it, she and I,

116

and she warned me to be careful. For you will kill me, too, if you can.'

'No!' Annalie sat up suddenly, wide-eyed. 'Lucinda, what are you saying?'

'What I shall say for everyone to hear,' her sister replied, fixing me with a look of hatred. 'I do not care to end up like Sophie, murdered by someone who will never be found, murdered by the lover of our dear Georgiana.'

I stood up, shaking with fury. 'How dare you say these things? It is not true, none of it. You were the one who spoke of suffocation. How can I tell that you did not plan this just to get rid of me? You hate me enough, and you hated Sophie, too.'

'No! It is you who hated Sophie. And I wish I had . . .'

She stopped as the door opened and Piers came in, to stare at the strange tableau we made, Lucinda and I facing each other with open hostility, Annalie huddled into herself, weeping.

'What's this?' Piers demanded. 'Haven't we enough trouble without petty squabbling?'

'Petty?' Lucinda cried. 'Here is the centre of the trouble. Your wife-to-be, Piers. Ask her what she was doing last night, while her lover pressed the life out of Sophie. Or perhaps she herself held the pillow. I would . . .'

'Enough!' Piers roared. 'You're babbling, Lucinda. Do you seriously accuse Georgiana of . . .'

'Of lies and deception. Yes. Of agreeing to marry you under false pretences. Of plotting cold-blooded murder. Oh, she will lie, but I know the truth. Sophie knew it, too. That is why she is dead. If I do not speak up I shall be next.'

Piers was obviously shocked and bewildered. 'Georgiana . . .'

'I can only repeat that none of this is true,' I said wretchedly. 'Lucinda accused me of it once before. She hates me because she is lame, and she has convinced herself that these lies are truth. If she is honest she will admit that the only person in this house to have attempted murder is herself.'

'See how she lies!' Lucinda cried, pointing an accusing finger at me. 'This is how she plans to discredit me. She says that I attacked her in the stable, that it was not the horse who injured her. Piers, you know that cannot be true. You know how helpless I am.'

'Then how do you know what I plan to say?' I demanded. 'We have not met since that day.'

'You said it just now, before Piers came in. Annalie will be my witness.'

Annalie raised a tear-stained face, blinking miserably. 'I wasn't really listening. I did hear you say something about the stables, Georgiana. I'm sorry, but I must tell the truth.'

'This is madness!' Piers said. 'You are all overwrought. Accusing each other of terrible things . . . I won't have it. If father hears any of

118

this nonsense it will be the end of him. Have a little consideration and wait a few days. If you still think there are things to be explained we shall go into it when we are all of a calmer mind.'

'Then I shall be careful to lock my door,' Lucinda said. 'I do not feel safe with this murderess running loose.'

Suddenly it was too much for me. I brushed past Piers and ran to my room, where I lay on the bed weeping for my friend Sophie and for all the bright dreams which now lay around me in ruins.

I had done with my tears and was sitting by the window watching the rain come endlessly down on the moor when Piers came to my door.

'I've been talking to Lucinda,' he told me gravely. 'It is all nonsense, of course, these things she accuses you of. I know that you have nothing to do with the Wolf ... May I come in?'

It was not proper for us to be alone in my room, but who was there to know or care on that day? I moved away from the door and returned to the window, leaning on the sill with my forehead against the cold glass. It gave me a little relief for my thudding headache.

'As to the other business,' Piers said, coming to stand behind me, 'I am at a loss to understand your motives. What did happen in the stable?'

'Lucinda and I argued. She held me prisoner with her crutch and when I tried to get away she almost fell. She dropped the stick. That much is true. But we were not in the stall. I was picking up the crutch for her when she hit me with a lantern.'

'Then how did you get into the stall?'

'She must have dragged me. Fright can give a person more than normal strength. It would not have been impossible for her.'

He was silent for a long moment before saying slowly, 'If this is true, why have you not told me before?'

'I didn't want to make trouble. I believed she had done it in a moment of uncontrollable rage that would probably never repeat itself. I thought if I could talk to her calmly I could make her see how wrong she was. But clearly I was mistaken.'

'It might have been possible, if Sophie had not interfered.'

I turned then, to look at him in dull surprise. 'Sophie? Oh, Piers, you can't believe that.'

'I only know what Lucinda told me—that she spoke to Sophie of her doubts and Sophie encouraged them.'

'That doesn't make sense. Why would she tell Sophie . . .' I paused, remembering the day when Lucinda had asked for someone to accompany her to the stable. It *had* been out of character for her to want me to go with her.

Had Sophie noticed, and questioned Lucinda afterwards? I could imagine the conversation. Sophie would have teased and prodded until she had the truth. But to have encouraged Lucinda in her wild fantasies . . . ? Why should Sophie have done that? Was she playing another of her games, pitting one against the other because she was bored?

'You have the answer?' Piers said.

'No. But I can see how it might have happened. When I saw Sophie last night she did say something which made me think she might know more than she pretended to.'

'Then you guessed that she and Lucinda might have discussed you?'

'No. It was not as clear as that, just a passing . . .' I looked at him sharply. 'You don't think I had anything to do with Sophie's death, do you?'

Lifting a hand to stroke my hair, Piers smiled at me. 'No, my love, I do not. Nor does anyone else seriously think so.'

'Except Lucinda.'

'Georgiana, we all know who killed Sophie. When he is found, even Lucinda will know that she has been wrong. But meanwhile I want you to go away from here . . . No. This time there will be no argument. You will leave on the next coach for London. The Wolf may not make a mistake a second time.'

'Mistake? You think he . . .'

'Yes, my darling.' His arms came about me,

pulling me close. 'It might have been you and not Sophie lying dead now. I'm sure it was you he came for, but as he searched for your room he disturbed Sophie and had to kill her to prevent her raising the alarm. That must be what happened. You are not safe here. You must go away until he is caught.'

'But Piers . . .'

He stopped my protests by putting his lips on mine, his hands caressing my waist and shoulders. It was not the time for love-making and I turned my head away, wondering how Piers could behave like that while Sophie lay below waiting for her coffin.

'I shall hate to be away from you,' he murmured in my ear. 'Let us have something to remember, Georgiana, until we are together again.'

Realizing that I was being propelled towards the bed, I twisted away from him, sick with revulsion. 'No! Have you no respect for the dead?'

Piers sat down on the edge of the bed. 'I'm sorry. For a moment I forgot . . . I love you so much, Georgiana. Why can't we comfort each other?'

'We can. But not that way.'

He stared at me, his expression derisive. 'It is the oldest way known for a woman to comfort a man. You forget that I am grieving for Sophie, too. I was fond of her, and I know my father adored her. I came to you for help.

Your arms could soothe me if they cared to. But what do you know of love? You are cold, Georgiana. When I touch you I feel you recoil. If you loved me you would not be so unkind.'

'Perhaps that is the trouble,' I said quietly, steeling myself for another unpleasant scene. 'It will be as well if I leave and do not come back. Lucinda was partly right about me, Piers. Marriage to you would mean security, and material things I shall never acquire on my own. But I don't love you as you want me to.'

For a moment he looked stricken, and then he sighed, coming to his feet and reaching for my hands.

'We are all saying things we do not mean,' he said sadly. 'Of course you love me. If not entirely, that will come when we are married. It is the way with most people . . . Forgive me. And never again speak of leaving for ever. One day soon you will return to Moorhollow as my wife. It may have to be delayed because of this tragedy over Sophie, but I will not let it be too long. That is a solemn promise.'

'I still think . . .' I began.

'No, Georgiana. I do not intend to argue. You will take the coach for London and stay with your sister until I come for you. Remember I have your promise. You wear my ring as a token.' He lifted my hand and kissed the fingers, his eyes on my face.

When Piers had gone I sat down in a chair and thought deeply about our relationship. He had shrugged aside the matter of Lucinda's hatred as though it was of no importance. Perhaps, to him, it was a petty woman's argument that would pass.

There was, of course, the strong possibility that soon Lucinda would marry and leave Moorhollow. With Lucinda gone and the Wolf safely in an asylum, or executed for murder, my future at Delfdale would be secure. But even then . . .

Belatedly, I made myself face the truth. I no longer wanted to be the wife of Piers Cheviot. In part, Lucinda had read me correctly, though it was not so simple as she appeared to think. I was worse than a mere fortune-hunter. A woman who married for gain could at least be honest with herself, but I had not even that saving grace. I had seen Piers' physical attractions and persuaded myself that admiration was love, all the time knowing that he could give me a comfortable life. But now I saw that what I felt for Piers fell far short of love. There were moments when I actually despised his weaknesses. It was no way for a woman to feel about the man she intended to marry.

As soon as I reached this conclusion there was further cause for shame, for I realized that I did not have the courage to try again to end the sham that our engagement had become. A governess to turn down the handsome heir to Moorhollow? The outrage, the recriminations, the hurt … I could not face it. Perhaps if Sophie had been alive I might have done it, but with everyone in deep shock after her death I had no right to inflict further trouble. And, being brutally honest with myself, I admitted that I did not care to leave Moorhollow under a cloud of disgrace.

To bare one's soul and find there the vices of pride and cowardice, never before fully acknowledged, is a chastening experience. My parents, I thought, had known me well, but I had ignored their warnings and gone my own way. Now I found myself in a trap of my own making.

This mood of depression stayed with me for the rest of that day, helped along by the dull headache which never quite left me. I considered the pain as part of the punishment.

In truth, I was too much occupied with myself. It is not a healthy pastime.

Consequently, when Mr Cheviot asked to see me the next morning I had no idea of his purpose. I had failed to ponder what the other members of the household were doing and saying, but within minutes of reaching the library I knew that Lucinda, at least, had not been idle.

Mr Cheviot sat at his desk, a tired shadow of his former bluff self. Nor did he ask me to take a seat, so I stood before him like a child brought to be reprimanded.

'I don't wish to make this a long interview,'

he said, supporting his head on one hand and staring at his desk. 'You may as well know that my daughter has been telling me some disquieting things about you. You know what those things are.'

'Yes,' I said.

He lifted his head to me, his small eyes blood-shot and swollen. 'What I want to know, Georgiana, is . . . is there any truth in it?'

'None.'

'You did not come here with the intention of capturing my son?'

'I did not. I came here as a companion to your wife and I was exceedingly grateful to you for the chance to be of service. I was very fond of your wife.'

'And also fond of my son?'

I hesitated, then said slowly, 'I thought so.'

His eyes narrowed to slits. 'Explain that.'

'Piers is . . . very handsome, and charming. When such a man paid court to me I was flattered, as any woman would be. I let myself believe that I loved him . . . It was wrong of me, but it was not planned. Your son made the advances. If he had not, the possibility would never have entered my mind. Why should it, when he could have any woman he chooses?'

'He chose you.'

I lowered my eyes, my face hot with shame. 'It seems so. But now that I have seen the truth of my own feelings I can no longer pretend. If you wish me to speak to Piers . . .'

126

'No.' The word came out on a long sigh. 'Not now. There is too much ... I must ask you frankly, Georgiana—do you know this man they call the Wolf?'

'No, sir.'

We surveyed each other, he searching my face gravely. 'And you had nothing to do with ... with what happened last night?'

'Nothing! As God is my witness ...'

'Very well,' he interrupted wearily. 'I believe you, Georgiana. Clearly my daughter has imagined her charges against you. But I think you will agree that the sooner you leave Moorhollow the better it will be for all of us.'

'Yes,' I said sadly.

'There will be a coach for London passing along the top road tomorrow. You will be taken to meet it. Go as though you intended to return, and when a decent interval has elapsed write to Piers and explain the situation. Perhaps once you are gone his feelings will change. I hope so.' He rubbed his face with his hands and continued in a dull voice, 'Do you still maintain that Lucinda attacked you?'

Again I hesitated. The poor man had enough on his mind. Why had Lucinda not waited until her father was more able to cope with these complications?

'Does she admit that she did?' I asked.

'She says you invented the story to discredit her. Piers says that only your generosity prevented you from telling the truth ... I confess, Georgiana, I am scarce able to think. I was shocked to hear my daughter speaking as she did. I had no idea there was such antipathy between you. But if she did injure you, and lie about it . . .'

'My leaving will surely solve that problem, too,' I said. It was not an answer to his question, but he did not seem to notice the omission. I think he already knew what was the truth. 'I'm sorry to have caused you so much distress,' I added quietly, 'especially at this time.'

'Troubles never come singly, so they say,' he muttered. 'You may go, Georgiana. And take everything with you. You are welcome to the clothes for the happiness you brought to . . . to Sophie.' His voice broke on the name. He buried his face in his hands. And I left the room, my eyes stinging with tears.

*   *   *

Next morning, as I checked my bedroom for any small things I might have left behind, Annalie came softly in and stood watching me mournfully.

'I shall miss you, Georgiana.'

'And I you. But we will write to each other. Here . . .' I opened my reticule and took out a piece of paper. 'Here is my sister's address. Will you keep me informed of everything that happens?'

'If I can. Papa is making arrangements for us to go his sister in Durham as soon as poor Sophie is laid to rest. He is afraid the Wolf might try to harm us all now that he has turned murderer. And to think we actually met the man ...' The memory made her eyes round with terror. 'He might have killed us then, both of us ... Oh, I'm glad that you will be safe.'

Together we went down to the hall, where Mr Cheviot shook my hand solemnly and said goodbye. I kissed Annalie and went out into the misty morning to where the carriage was waiting, with Piers standing by it.

'All is ready,' he said. 'If the Wolf dares to try to take you he is in for a surprise. I have a pistol and the coachman has a shotgun.'

'Do you think such precautions are necessary?' I asked.

Piers shrugged. 'Perhaps not. But I am taking no chances. Now that he has struck he has nothing to lose by striking again.'

I no longer knew what to think. Was the Wolf mad? Was he a murderer? Or was it all fabrication, a cover for something of which I was entirely ignorant? But what did it matter to me now? I was going away from it all. Perhaps I would never learn the truth.

Instead of lifting, the morning mist thickened into fog. It was impossible to see more than a few yards, but as we passed through the village I could make out the

129

shapes of the houses and knew that we were climbing from the valley to the high road from where I had first admired the moors.

Beside me, Piers sat alertly, watching the shifting fog. Every few minutes his hand slid to a bulge beneath his coat, where he kept the pistol. Neither of us had much to say.

I was tired, having spent a sleepless night, and my head still pounded with a nagging ache which the motion of the coach did nothing to allay. The thought of the journey, long days in a stage-coach and nights in noisy inns, was not a pleasant one.

After an hour's slow journey through the featureless greyness we came to a deserted cross-roads on the moor. The heavy mist lay over everything like a blanket, making the world so silent that my ears sang with it.

'This must be farewell, Georgiana,' Piers said, taking my gloved hand in his. 'But not for long. I shall come for you as soon as is possible.'

I nodded, unable to find any words. There was nothing to say.

The coachman was lifting down my valises, leaving them by the side of the main road. I saw him lifting his head, listening.

'The stage-coach is coming, sir,' he called.

'It's in good time,' Piers said, consulting his watch. 'Perhaps it's as well. I don't like saying goodbye to you.'

He kissed me, briefly but with great passion,

and held my arm tightly as he helped me alight.

I could hear the thunder of approaching hooves and the creaking of a vehicle, jingling harness. Out from the mist the four horses emerged, pulling the swaying coach. It stopped just beyond us and one of the men in the box leaped down to assist our coachman with my baggage.

Piers opened the door, murmuring, 'Remember I love you. Wait for me, my dearest,' and handed me into the coach.

There was only one other passenger, a grim-faced woman who held a basket on her lap. I bade her, 'Good morning,' and she inclined her head coldly, glowering beyond me to where Piers was standing bare-headed in the mist.

He looked worried, I thought with a pang of regret. How different he was from the carefree young man I had met in London. As the coach set off he lifted his hat in farewell and I waved a reply. But I felt no emotion. I was leaving Delfdale for good.

Turning away from the desolate scene outside, I met the cold eyes of my fellow-passenger. Had I been feeling better I might have made some attempt to draw her into conversation, but I had neither the will nor the energy. Fate had caught up with me again, was pulling me back to the preordained road from which I had so nearly escaped.

My thoughts turned to the immediate future. Christina would be pleased to see me and would probably welcome my help for a few months. I could take care of the three small children and do unskilled chores on the farm. But Christina's husband would not welcome me as a permanent resident in his home, nor could I consider it as anything other than a temporary expedient. Perhaps I could become a schoolteacher.

Worn out in mind, body and spirit, I let my heavy eyelids close and fell into a shallow, dream-filled sleep.

*   *   *

The drumming of the wheels over cobbles awakened me. I saw that the coach was passing through a gateway in high walls.

An inn, already? I thought dazedly, sitting up and peering out.

It was indeed a yard of some kind. There were stables and outhouses set around the cobbled area. I heard dogs barking. Some of them came into sight. Big, grey, wolf-like . . .

No!

My heart began to hammer in alarm as the dogs leapt joyfully in greeting around the man who climbed from the driver's seat. He patted each in turn, then swung round to open the door of the coach, taking off the wide-brimmed hat he wore.

With a tight, humourless smile, the Wolf said, 'Welcome to Wierdmoor House, Miss Forrest.'

CHAPTER NINE

Unable to believe that I was not still dreaming, I glanced at the other woman in the coach, only to find her regarding me calmly. This was no surprise to her.

'Come down,' the Wolf said. 'Don't worry about the dogs. They won't harm you . . . Oh, very well. Let me help you, Mrs Thomas. Our guest appears to want to remain in the coach for a while.'

'Guest?' I said sharply as the woman climbed down.

'Indeed. You will stay with us a while now that you're here, won't you?'

'Do I have a choice?' I asked.

'Certainly. Come in the house or stay in the coach. As you please. Though the coach is going nowhere except into the coachhouse, I assure you. You will be warmer in the house. Mrs Thomas has gone to prepare luncheon. Aren't you hungry?'

Unwillingly, and avoiding the hand he held out, I stepped down from the vehicle. The dogs came round me, curious, but at a word from their master all sat docilely.

I glanced round the yard. The high wall surrounded everything and the gates were now closed. I was securely imprisoned.

'This way,' said the Wolf, taking my arm in a firm grip.

As we rounded the coach I saw the house for the first time, a tall, gaunt place with twin towers reaching up into the mist. And from somewhere came a distant booming which I eventually identified as breakers crashing on a shore.

Molly's words came back to me—a black castle on tall cliffs where the moors meet the sea. A wild, lonely place. Who had known enough to start that rumour, which was very near the truth?

The Wolf led me into the house via a long dark passageway which led into a stone-flagged hall. The chill of the place made me shiver.

'It's always cold in here,' my captor told me, 'but there's a fire in your room.'

I was taken up the stairs and along a corridor to a room whose door stood open invitingly. The bed was prepared and a bright fire burned in the grate.

In the doorway I drew back, looking up at that face which had once been handsome. The Wolf's eyes were glittering with maleficent humour.

'Afraid, Miss Forrest? Do not be. You are to be my guest until certain matters have been

134

resolved to my satisfaction. That is all.'

'How can I believe that?' I demanded. 'You have abducted me.'

'Ah, but no-one knows that. No-one knows where you are. Not even Piers Cheviot, who so kindly gave you into my hands.'

'And you think you can kill me without . . .'

'Kill you?' His face darkened terribly and his voice was grim. 'Miss Forrest, I do not kill women. Not with pillows in the night or any other means.'

'Then how do you know . . .'

'I know many things. I do not exactly understand what has been happening at Moorhollow, but you and I will discover the truth together . . . You may as well rest until the meal is ready. You will hear the gong. The dining-room is to the right of the hall. I shall ask Henry to bring your luggage to you.'

With that he strode away, leaving me standing in the doorway of the room which had been made ready for me, still a little frightened but more bewildered. Why had he brought me here?

There was no key in the lock, so I could not lock myself, or be locked, in. All the same, I was a prisoner.

A few moments later a grizzled, wind-browned man brought my valises and stood them by the wall.

'Are you Henry?' I asked.

'Yes, miss.' He touched his forelock as if I

were gentry, regarding me with a look of polite enquiry.

'What does your master want with me?'

'I think you better ask *him* that, miss. But one thing's sure—he won't harm you. Whoever's telling them wicked lies about him ought to be shot. Will that be all, miss?'

The Wolf had loyal servants, I thought. Henry, and the woman who had ridden in the coach, who must be the cook. There was another thing of which I was now sure—most definitely the Wolf was not a madman. Even from our alarming meeting in the lane I had judged that correctly. And yet Piers insisted that his enemy was insane.

It must be, I realized with a shock, that Piers had lied to me every time the subject of the Wolf was mentioned. But why? What did he wish to hide?

Taking off my coat, hat and gloves, I sat down by the fire to wrestle mentally with the problem, but it did no good.

Perhaps half an hour later I heard a gong being struck three times. As the notes died away along the corridor I ventured forth, knowing that the mystery would only be solved by another meeting with the Wolf.

He was already in the dining-room, staring morosely out of the window at the unmoving mist and as I entered I saw his face in profile. The scar was hidden from that side. Aquiline nose and firm chin dominated his features, giving him a look of strength, and dark sidewhiskers grew almost to his jaw-line. Seen like that, in a mulberry-coloured coat and white shirt with a silk cravat at his throat, it was difficult to believe that he was the same man who rode the moors in a hooded burnous.

He turned, and immediately the picture was marred by that awful scar.

'You came, then.' It was a flat statement. 'I thought perhaps you might stay in your room and refuse to come out.'

'Since there is no key, I could not have prevented you from fetching me,' I said.

A sardonic smile twisted his mouth. 'You misjudge me, Miss Forrest. If I had wanted to harm you I could have done so many times these past weeks. It is not for that reason I brought you here, but perhaps only time will convince you of that. Sit down and let us eat.'

The woman from the stage-coach had come in with a tureen from which she began to serve steaming hot game soup.

'This is my housekeeper Mrs Thomas,' the Wolf told me. 'She and her husband manage to cope with this house and the stables, and me. I'm afraid we live very frugally. Do not expect the lavish comforts you enjoyed at Moorhollow.'

'One does not expect much from a prison,' I said sourly.

'A prison?' Dark eyebrows rose. 'Mrs Thomas, is Miss Forrest our prisoner?'

'She might think so,' the housekeeper replied in a tone I had never encountered from a servant to her master. 'I don't suppose she understands what it's all about, not yet. But don't you worry, miss. You're in no danger.'

Having finished with serving the soup, she departed.

'Why *did* you bring me here?' I asked.

He looked at me for a long, silent moment before replying slowly, 'It's what I have been planning all this last long year. To take Piers Cheviot's woman and ...' He broke off, shaking his head. 'But after I had met you it was not quite so simple.'

'Why do you hate Piers so much?'

'Because he took my wife from me, Miss Forrest. And having taken her, he destroyed her.' His voice was dark and I found myself staring into savage black eyes, while a pulse thudded painfully in my temple. Was this why Piers had lied to me?

Despite myself, the memory of that day in the lane returned vividly. The Wolf had said he would do to Piers what Piers had done to him. I understood now why I was involved, and I remembered all too clearly that ferocious embrace he had forced on me, as a 'sample'.

His mouth bent into that crooked, bitter smile. 'Your face is expressive, Miss Forrest. But once again I assure you that you need have no fear of me. I have to reconsider my

138

plans. The ravishment of an imaginary woman was easy enough to plan, but to force myself on someone whom I know, someone whom I admire . . . I could not do it. I find that I have too much respect for you. Indeed, whoever the woman had been it would have ended the same way. The theory could never be put into practice. I am not an animal . . . But the soup will be cold. Eat, Miss Forrest.'

To my surprise I found that I was hungry. The fare was plain but cooked to perfection and delicious. Afterwards we moved to the Wolf's study, it being the only other room with a fire, he told me. It was a small, warm room, the fire burning brightly, lightening the gloom caused by the mist outside.

I sat in one of the chairs by the hearth, while the Wolf took a long cigar from a silver box on the desk and made a business of lighting it.

'You live here alone?' I asked, finding myself more curious than afraid. The continued assurances that I was in no danger were beginning to take effect.

'Except for Henry and Mrs Thomas, yes. My parents died some years ago.' This with a gesture to the two portraits on the side wall. 'Oh—forgive me, Miss Forrest. You do not object if I smoke?'

'You forget that I am your prisoner,' I said.

'My guest,' he replied firmly. 'But I fear you must remain so until I have settled matters with Piers Cheviot.'

'Piers swore to me that he did not know you,' I said.

'Did he?' Grim amusement lit his eyes. 'I wondered what ploy he would use. Did you believe him?'

'Not entirely. But I could see no reason for him to lie . . . He told me you were insane.'

'Do you think he is right?'

'Not now. At Moorhollow I did not know what to think. Everyone firmly believed what Piers said. And your behaviour has served to add credence to it.'

'Prowling the moors with my "wolves", you mean?' he asked.

'Yes. That, and the stupid way you accosted Annalie and myself.'

He was surprised by that. 'Stupid?'

'Blind anger is stupid, and so is the wish for revenge. If you must punish Piers you should have the courage to . . .'

'I did,' he interrupted in a hard voice. 'After Jane died I went out of my way to meet him. I had him at my feet, with a pistol at his head. But then I wondered why I should risk the gallows for him. He is not worth it. So I let him go, but I warned him that he should be careful never to care deeply for any woman, for if he did he would regret it. I promised him to take her and use her as he used Jane. And at the time I meant it. That day when I stopped you it was my intention to remind him of it, in case he had forgotten, an attempt to frighten you

140

away. But you do not frighten so easily, it seems.'

'I did not realize, then, that I was a pawn in your game. And what do you intend to do with me now?'

The Wolf shrugged. 'Only keep you here, and let him know that I have you. His imagination will do the rest. He should learn what it is to suffer, as Jane suffered.'

'You still have not told me exactly what Piers is supposed to have done,' I said.

'Supposed? You think I would go to these lengths for an imagined wrong?' He threw himself down in the chair opposite mine. 'Very well, Miss Forrest. But it is not a pleasant story. You wear his ring. You are intending to marry him. Do you care to have your illusions shattered?'

'After the way you have treated me, I think I have a right to know.'

'As you say . . . First I must tell you about my wife. She was the only daughter of elderly parents. Her two brothers were years older than she was. So you can imagine that she had been adored and given everything she wanted . . . I met her when she came to stay at York with some cousins. She was bored and looking for adventure, though I did not realize it at the time. I fell in love with her. We were married. A big gathering, of course. She enjoyed being the centre of all attention. And so we came here.'

As he paused, he stood up restlessly, remaining with his back to the fire, towering over me.

'She disliked the house from the beginning,' he continued. 'It was too big, too empty, too cold, too far away from what she thought of as life. I thought she would settle. Much could be done to improve this house. But Jane was not interested in anything other than parties and gossip, new clothes and people to admire her. She had few housewifely talents. Knowing she was not happy, I did not object when she took to riding alone on the moors. It seemed to please her. She always came back with bright eyes and a smile on her lips.' He glanced down at me. 'You can guess why.'

'Piers?' I queried, feeling chilled.

He nodded slowly, his mouth compressed. 'Piers Cheviot. When and how she met him I do not know. I knew him only slightly myself. But Jane did meet him. Somewhere on the moors, about halfway between here and Moorhollow, there is an old shepherd's hut. It was a meeting-place for them all that summer. And I did not suspect, even when she began to bar her door to me. But that made me angry. We quarrelled about it. Violently. One night at dinner ...' His hands were fists, his jaw clenched as he relived the scene. 'She jumped up, took hold of the carving knife. Struck!' His arm flew up as if to ward off a blow, and his hand came to rest on his cheek where the scar

142

was so that I could imagine what he had not put into words.

'You told me it was Piers who wounded you,' I said in a hushed voice.

His hand fell slowly and he glanced at me darkly. 'No, Miss Forrest. I believe I said that I had Piers Cheviot to thank for it, which is true, since he was the one who put the idea of killing me into Jane's mind.'

I stared at him, horrified. Piers had done that? Seduced this man's wife and then suggested she kill her husband?

'When she saw what she had done, she broke down,' the Wolf went on, his voice toneless now. 'She confessed her affair with Piers. He had told her that he would marry her if she were free. And naturally she believed it. He is plausible, is he not, and exceedingly skilled in pleasing women? Charming? Everything I am not. Everything she wanted. So I told her to go to him, and she went. All she had left me was this! Even the doctor's wife near fainted at sight of me. Other women shrieked. Men stared. Do you wonder I took to keeping my own company?'

Silently, I shook my head.

He sighed heavily and continued with his story, 'A year passed. I had no word from Jane and I avoided any encounter with Cheviot. If I had seen him I would have killed him . . . Then I had a letter from my wife's cousins in York. Jane was there, about to have a child. She had told them not to get in touch with me, but they did so anyway. They were very worried about her. Jane was ill, very ill. Thin. Unkempt . . . I discovered that Cheviot had found her lodgings in a fishing village, where he could visit her. And then he stopped going without any warning. When Jane realized her condition she wrote and begged him for help. And he replied. I have the letter, if you wish to see it.'

He strode across to his desk, jerked open a drawer and took out an envelope which he gave to me. With fumbling hands I took out the letter. There was no doubt that Piers had written it.

I read: Madam, I am in receipt of your communication. If you do not cease to annoy me with your importuning I shall have no choice but to take your letter to a magistrate. Is there any proof that the child you are carrying is mine? I assure you that you will find no-one to say that I ever visited you. You are an adulteress and a blackmailer and I shall not be inveigled into acknowledging your bastard as my own. The penalty for libel is harsh, as you will discover if ever you attempt to contact me again.

Wordlessly, I returned the letter to the Wolf.

'Of course,' he said, 'Cheviot was gambling that Jane would be too ashamed to take the matter to the law. If she had, he might have

144

found difficulty in explaining this letter, though it is couched in ambiguous terms. Jane asked in the village where she was staying, but no-one would admit the identity of her lover. Cheviot had paid them well to keep his secret ... The hag she was staying with, knowing that Jane was in deep trouble, began to demand her rent, so in desperation Jane wrote to her cousins. One of them went to rescue her and in turn sent for me ... Can you imagine my feelings when I found her in that state? She had killed everything I had felt for her, but she was still my wife. Out of pity, I offered to take her back.'

He stopped, his face twisting, and the silence lengthened.

'Did she come?' I ventured at last.

A short, bitter laugh escaped him. 'No, Miss Forrest. She said, "You? It was torture living with you before. I could never live with you now. You're hideous, hateful, ugly" ... It was the last time I saw her. She took her own life. A knife again. Through her wrists. And she died with his name on her lips, so they told me.

'That is why I hate Piers Cheviot. I wanted to kill him, but when I had the chance I changed my mind. Some day, I knew, there would be a woman he truly cared about. And when that happened I would take her and degrade her as he did to Jane.' He looked down at me, the anger dying on his face. 'That was my plan, Miss Forrest. I dreamed of it for a year, growing obsessed with it. And then I saw you on the moor that day, tending that hoyden of a girl after the accident she so richly deserved. I thought you were splendid, so when I heard you planned to marry him I was doubly furious. A woman like you, to waste yourself ... Perhaps I *was* on the verge of madness. I had lived with the thought of revenge, with bitter hatred in my heart ... Can you understand that?'

'I think so.'

Sighing heavily, the Wolf lowered himself into the chair and bent to stab at the fire with a poker, sending a shower of sparks up the chimney.

'I had reckoned without other forces,' he said. 'I learned that you had been badly hurt by Lucinda and I found that I was ...'

I caught my breath sharply. 'You knew about that? But no-one ... Unless ... The stable-lad?'

'He is the Thomases' son. He took work at Moorhollow and has been reporting events to me. He was a witness to what occurred. Why did you not tell someone the truth?'

'I did, yesterday. But there is so much other trouble that ...'

'Ah, yes. The late Mrs Cheviot. I ask you, Miss Forrest, when the damning evidence was discovered, why did Piers not immediately tell the constable where I could be found?'

'He couldn't, unless he told the full story.

He has sworn all along that he does not know who you are, or where you live. But if *you* did not kill Sophie, then who . . .'

The Wolf smiled his sardonic smile. 'That, Miss Forrest, is what I should like to know.'

CHAPTER TEN

Being with the Wolf, watching his face as he talked, I had no choice but to accept that everything he had told me was the truth. He was not a bad man, but a bitterly hurt one, with wounds that went far deeper than the scar which made him so self-conscious.

That evening we ate dinner together in a more relaxed atmosphere. Candles gleamed between us, in a three pronged silver candelabrum, and the very house felt more friendly now that the curtains were drawn, shutting out the enveloping mist.

'What are your plans now?' the Wolf asked. I had told him of the events at Moorhollow since my arrival.

'I shall go to my sister's home in Kent, and from there seek employment.'

'You won't go back to Moorhollow?'

'I did not intend to. I had doubts about Piers even before I came here, and now that I know what he really is . . .'

'What kind of doubts?'

I looked down at my water-glass, turning it between my fingers. 'It is difficult to express. In the beginning I felt that he was not sincere, but he persuaded me otherwise and latterly he changed and seemed to be honest in his desire to protect me. But I always felt dissatisfied after we had spoken about ... about you. I could not crystallize the feeling, nor did I try very hard, for I had convinced myself I loved him. I suspected him of lying but could not understand why he should do so. And there were moments when things he said and did were overstated ... I can't explain it more clearly. I only faced up to it two days ago, and knew that I could never marry him.'

'Did you tell him so?' the Wolf asked sharply.

Puzzled by his tone, I looked across the table and saw that he was frowning.

'No. I did try once, but he would not listen. And with all the grief over Sophie I did not want to inflict further trouble. I shall write and tell him how I feel when the family have had time to ...' I paused, realizing that the situation was changed. 'Perhaps I shall not need to write.'

'He believes you will go back to him?'

'He has no reason to think otherwise.' As I watched the frown clear from his face I suddenly understood the reasons for his questions. If Piers did not love me, the revenge would not work.

'What do you expect him to do when he knows I am here?' I asked.

The Wolf shook his head and rose from the chair to fetch a cigar from a box on the side-table. 'I don't know. He may come here to rescue you. If he does, you can tell him to his face that your engagement is ended. That will satisfy me.'

As he leaned towards the candelabrum to light his cigar, I watched his face. He was still a young man, but there were lines of bitterness about his mouth and furrowing his brow, those and that dreadful scar ... Mephistopheles, I thought.

'You find me horrific?' he asked flatly.

'No.' It was the truth.

'And why not? My own wife did. But naturally she knew me when I could still look the world in the eye with equanimity.'

'Don't you now?'

He laughed shortly, throwing himself back into his chair. 'Most of the time I can, when I am among men I know. But in mixed company ... If you were not thinking about that, what was in your mind?'

'I was thinking that the quest for revenge is an unworthy occupation for a man like yourself. You have wasted a year on it, but even when it is complete ... even if you send Piers to perdition, it will not bring your wife back, or heal that scar.'

'No, but it might save some other woman

from a fate similar to Jane's. Piers Cheviot needs to be taught a lesson.'

'The law could have done that for you,' I said.

'Not in the way I want it done.'

'Then it is for yourself you will do it. Because *you* have been hurt.'

He leaned back in his chair, a faint smile curving his lips. 'Are you reprimanding me, Miss Forrest? I have already modified my plans for your benefit. You should by now be a quivering wreck, but I have not touched you. Of course, Piers does not know that. He will assume that the worst has happened, as I told him it would if he was ever so thoughtless as to bring a woman for whom he . . .'

I did not hear the rest of the sentence, for something he had said turned a key in my memory. Why had it not done so before? He had told me often enough that Piers was fully aware of his intentions.

I was seeing Piers' face as I had seen it that first time, when I was drenched in Lady Teignford's perfume. Blue eyes. Surprise, interest, speculation . . . And later, when his father and Sophie had agreed to employ me . . .

'What's wrong?' the Wolf asked, breaking into my thoughts as he leaned on the table.

'I've just realized . . .' I breathed. 'My predicament made me easy prey. He knew I would grasp any chance, would be grateful to him. Yes! And then . . .'

'Miss Forrest,' my host said patiently. 'I do not follow you. Your predicament?'

'I'm sorry . . . I was a governess, and Piers witnessed my dismissal. It was unjust, but it left me with little hope of a similar post. As I left the house, Piers met me and told me his stepmother had need of a companion. I thought it a strange way to employ anyone, but I went with him. When his father agreed to take me, Piers looked very . . . "triumphant" is the only word for it. But I was so pleased to have found a situation that . . .'

'He began to court you almost at once?'

'As soon as we were at Moorhollow. The very first night. For a while I did not believe he could mean it, but when he actually proposed marriage . . .' I sighed, angry with myself. 'Fool that I was, I believed he really loved me.'

The Wolf was silent for a long time, his expression grim. 'I see,' he said eventually. 'He hoped that I would wreak my vengeance on you and be brought to book for it. That is how much he cares for you, Miss Forrest. He knew exactly what I intended. And you were the Judas-goat, staked out to trap the tiger—or, in this case, the Wolf!'

*   *   *

We removed once again to the study, which was cosy with the candlelight and a log fire

151

burning. The things I had learned about Piers made me sick, and angry. I, who had talked so pompously about revenge, would willingly have taken a knife to Piers myself if he had appeared at that moment.

But the peace of the study soon relaxed me. Piers would pay, in one way or another. Iniquity never prospered long.

'Forgive my asking,' I said as my host lowered his tall frame into the fireside chair, 'but may I know your name? I can no longer go on thinking of you as . . .'

'The Wolf?' he asked with amusement. 'An emotive name, probably invented because of my dogs. I wonder who first thought of it. Piers himself? But he knows my real name as well as his own. It is Marriott. Ethan Marriott.'

'Thank you.'

'Not at all. I should have introduced myself sooner, but I gave the matter no thought . . . Tell me, Miss Forrest, what are your thoughts about the second Mrs Cheviot? You were there in the house. Who would benefit by her death?'

'No-one at Moorhollow would do such a thing,' I said, though my tone expressed my doubt.

'No? But who else is there? Was Mrs Cheviot so very well-loved by every member of the family?'

'There was friction, of course. There was bound to be. She was not so much older than her step-daughters and had a mischievous turn of mind and an acid tongue when she chose. Lucinda despised her . . .'

'And we already know that Lucinda has a violent temper,' he put in.

'Yes. I did wonder . . . But to imagine her capable of murder . . .'

'What of Miss Annalie?'

I lifted my head, looking him in the eye and saying at once, 'It could not have been Annalie. She is a sweet, gentle girl.'

'But how did she feel about her step-mother?'

'She didn't say. She never said a harsh word against anyone. Even though Sophie was sometimes unkind to her . . .' I stopped, because the look on Ethan Marriott's face told me that he thought Annalie, too, might have a motive for murder.

'No!' I said forcefully. 'It was not Annalie, nor any of them.'

'Not even Piers?'

'Piers? What motive would he have? He has done many wicked things, but that . . . We are despicable, to be sitting here like this and gossiping about them.'

'But Mrs Cheviot *is* dead, is she not?'

'And will be buried tomorrow. She was my friend, Mr Marriott, and I cannot cold-bloodedly analyse what happened. She was human and had her faults, but nothing that would cause anyone to kill her. Her death makes no sense.'

'You're tired,' he said, his voice surprisingly gentle. 'Forgive me. I've been thoughtless. Why don't you go to your room now?'

He rose as I did, and bade me goodnight, but before I reached the door he spoke my name. I looked round, seeing that he was holding out a key.

'You may wish to lock your door,' he said, bringing the key to me. He placed it in my palm and wrapped my fingers round it, holding my hand in his own. 'Goodnight again. And thank you. It means a great deal to me to know that you trust me, after everything I have done to you. Am I forgiven?'

'Yes.' I could not look at him. His nearness discomposed me, but I had been unable to withdraw my hand from his gentle grip.

Very slowly, he uncurled his fingers, and said for a third time, 'Goodnight.'

'Goodnight,' I whispered, and fled.

When I reached my room a look in the glass told me that my face was scarlet. The past few hours had held much to horrify and annoy me, yet here I was blushing like an innocent because a man I hardly knew had touched me. Nor was it a blush of displeasure.

*   *   *

The sound of the sea lulled me to sleep and in the morning the gentle rush of waves greeted me. As I opened my eyes, wondering where I was, I saw sunlight pouring in a wide shaft through a gap in the curtains.

Today, I thought, Sophie will be laid in the ground. It still did not seem possible. She had been so bright, so full of life. How sad Mr Cheviot must be, and Annalie, Lucinda—and the detestable Piers, who had brought me to Moorhollow as a lamb to the butcher.

Remembering that, I was again angry. I would not rest until I had seen Piers and told him my opinion of his true character. The decision roused me from my bed.

I went to the window and found myself looking out across a small bay. The house stood on the lowest point of the curving cliffs but was still high above the rocks which formed the beach. I could see the edge of the cliff some fifty yards away.

A path of flat stones led towards the precipice from the house, set in well-kept lawns, the whole dotted with hardy shrubs, and beyond this pleasant cliff-top garden stretched the sea, creaming in sparkling waves across the rocky shore. I also saw that the entire area was surrounded by the high stone wall through which I had passed in the coach. It ended on a level with the rim of the cliff, making the house into a virtual fortress.

Ethan Marriott was already at breakfast, though he stood up as I entered and came to hold a chair for me. His manners, now, were impeccable.

'I hope you are rested,' he said as he returned to his place.

'Yes, thank you. I feel much better.'

His eyes searched my face, as though to judge for himself the state of my health. 'I'm afraid I shall have to be away for most of the day. Will you find a way to amuse yourself?'

'Do you really wish me to stay?'

'I thought we had agreed on it. You will remain here until we have dealt with Piers Cheviot once and for all.'

'Is that where you're going?' I asked in alarm.

A grim smile touched his mouth. 'Not yet. I have business to attend to. What will you do while I'm gone?'

'May I explore the house?'

'If you wish.'

'And go down to the beach—there is a path?'

'There is. Take the dogs with you, if you like. You are not afraid of them?'

'I don't think so. Will they come with me?'

'As long as you speak firmly to them.'

When we had eaten he took me out to the stable yard and there introduced me to his exuberant wolfhounds—Aries and Scamp, Dio, Trog, Djin and Flick. I said that I would never remember which was which, but he replied with a laugh that all answered to 'boy' when necessary. He also showed me the way he made them howl, by clicking his fingers and throwing back his own head. The resultant hullabaloo near deafened me.

'A childish trick!' he remarked, deriding himself. 'I thought to terrorise the whole Cheviot family.'

'You did,' I said. 'And me, too.'

He gave me a sorrowful look. 'I apologize. To you, at least. I wonder if the legend will remain when the Wolf no longer rides the moors.'

'It probably will. The wind makes a similar noise.'

'Does it?' The notion seemed to please him. 'Then I may acquire some measure of immortality.'

The black stallion was brought out and stood patiently waiting. Moving across to it, Ethan Marriott fastened the top frogging of the burnous he wore slung round his shoulders. Needless to say, there was no rent in the garment, no place where it had been mended.

But as he lifted the hood I was suddenly appalled and grasped his arm.

'Please! Don't wear that.'

'Why not?'

I had not thought why. It was simply that I hated to think of him returning to his other self.

'They are looking for you,' I said. 'If you go dressed like that . . .'

'Are you worried about me?' he asked, with that mocking lift of eyebrows.

'Yes, I am.'

'Then do not be. My business takes me miles away. None of the nearby villagers have ever known me as the Wolf. Since I was wounded I have kept away from them.'

I was still not happy but could not tell him so. Ethan Marriott was my friend. The Wolf was my enemy. It was a matter of feelings, not logical reasoning.

After watching me for a moment he strode away to the house and returned without the burnous, bringing instead a wide-brimmed hat which he donned at an acute angle so as to throw the scarred side of his face into shadow. He stood regarding me with a roguish twinkle in his eye.

'You're a dangerous woman, Miss Forrest,' he said as he stepped lightly to the saddle. 'I shall be back before dinnertime.'

The gates were opened and he rode away, leaving the dogs staring longingly after him. Feeling suddenly energetic, I ran to fetch my pelisse, called the dogs, and took them around the house and down by the cliff path. Most of the morning had gone by the time we returned from romping on the beach.

*   *   *

I spent the afternoon looking around the

house. It was very old, full of fascinating nooks and crannies and small passageways, but most of the rooms had a chill, musty feeling about them as though they had not been used for a long time. It was a great pity, for the dust covers hid some beautiful pieces of furniture, but I could well imagine the dismay of Ethan Marriott's young bride when she came to this house.

I thought a great deal about the Cheviots and wondered what was happening at Moorhollow, but no amount of pondering brought me the least clue as to the identity of Sophie's murderer. It must have been someone whose association with her I did not know, someone from her past, perhaps, but it had to be someone who was close enough to Moorhollow to know all about the Wolf and lay the blame at his door.

As it was, the police were still looking for the Wolf. They must know that their quarry had a scar on his face. Annalie had seen it. So if Ethan Marriott was seen he might be arrested. Would he be able to prove his innocence?

The hours went by and it grew dark. As the minutes ticked away I felt more and more concerned about my host and was eventually drawn to an upper window from where I could see the yard. Lanterns burned either side of the gateway, shining out through the gathering night as beacons, but beyond them lay mile after mile of empty moorland. If the police had caught him ... If he had encountered Piers ...

It was past eight when a rider galloped into the yard. The dogs grouped round him exuberantly and in relief I, too, went flying to meet him, though I collected myself when I reached the stairs and was walking calmly down them when he strode into the hall.

'I'm late,' he said, looking up at me with an apologetic smile. 'I hope you have not been concerned.'

'Not unduly,' I lied.

He offered a helping hand as I came down the last few stairs and I accepted it with what I hoped was an impersonal air. But the touch of his fingers thrilled me as it had before and he did not let me go.

'Is that why you were watching for me?' he asked. 'I could see you framed against the light as I rode up. And your hand is as cold as mine. How long have you been standing at the window?'

'Not long.' I lifted my head and saw the question in his eyes, which made it impossible for me to prevaricate longer. 'Of course I was worried!' I said heatedly. 'I thought you might have met Piers, or been arrested.'

'Arrested? On what charge?'

'You may have forgotten, but the police think that you killed Sophie Cheviot.'

Ethan Marriott laughed. 'Then let them

160

arrest me. I see I omitted to tell you, Georgiana. On the night when I supposedly entered Moorhollow by stealth I was staying with friends in York. I was in their company until two o'clock in the morning, and breakfasted with them at eight. No-one could have ridden to Delfdale and back in six hours.'

I was intensely relieved to hear it.

*   *   *

Across the candles at the dinner table, my host raised his glass in a silent toast.

'We may not have long to wait now,' he said. 'In a day or two Piers Cheviot will receive my letter.'

'You wrote to him?' I asked in astonishment.

'Of course. I want him to know that I am holding you here, locked in an attic, weeping and wailing for him, and no longer an undefiled maiden.' His mouth twitched humorously at my look of horror. 'No, Georgiana. I merely told him you were here. The rest he will imagine for himself.'

'But has it not occurred to you that, even when he knows, he will not come himself, he will send the police. It was for exactly that purpose he brought me to Moorhollow.'

'As a trap for me, yes. If he can prove that I kidnapped and assaulted you, he will be free of me. But I put no address on my letter. He can

161

tell no-one where I am without revealing his own mendacity. So I expect him to attempt a rescue single-handed ... I have given it much thought today. You said he seemed insincere at first but that he changed. And there is no doubt that recently he was most anxious for you to leave Moorhollow.'

'Yes,' I said, unable to follow his reasoning.

Ethan Marriott watched me across the rim of his glass for a moment. 'I suspect that he came to care for you. The lie turned into reality for him.'

I had not thought of that. I had only considered the callous way Piers had picked on me as suitable material for his purpose. But when I really recalled the way he had behaved latterly, I saw that it was possible that he had grown genuinely fond of me.

'Hoist with his own petard,' my host said with satisfaction. 'Poor Cheviot. I feel almost sorry for him.'

'What will you do if he comes?' I asked. 'There must be no violence.'

'Don't you want me to give him a beating?'

'It may be the other way around.'

The light in his eyes mocked me. 'Is your concern for me? I'm flattered.'

'He is not worth the trouble a fight may cause,' I countered. 'It would be more honest of us to go to Moorhollow and tell them the truth. Then some progress might be made in finding the person who killed Sophie. I am not concerned with revenge. If I had not been so gullible I would never have engaged myself to Piers. So it is partly my own fault.'

Moving the candelabrum to one side so that he could see me more clearly, Ethan Marriott leaned across the table and laid his hand over mine.

'We shall agree on a compromise, taking into account the family's bereavement. They must be allowed a few days' respite . . . If Piers does not come here within three days, you and I will call at Moorhollow and tell them everything we know, with the constable as a witness. Does that seem a reasonable course of action, Georgiana?'

'It does.'

'Good. Then that is what we shall do . . . Tell me, do you play chess?'

My father had taught me the game. It occupied the rest of the evening.

* * *

Unfortunately, though Ethan Marriott and I had discussed the most obvious possibilities, we had failed to read Piers' mind. He did not allow us three days, or even one.

We were finishing breakfast the next morning when Mrs Thomas came rushing in.

'He's here!' she gasped. 'At the gate. Piers Cheviot. He demands to see you, Mr Marriott.'

163

Her employer frowned. 'Already? But he can't possibly have received my letter ... All right, Mrs Thomas, I'll come.'

As he stood up I pushed back my chair and rose also, intending to go with him.

'No, Georgiana,' he said flatly. 'You stay inside. He can't know that you are here.'

'Then why has he come?'

The frown returned. 'I don't know. But I would prefer it if you did not go out there.'

'And I would prefer to hear what transpires,' I said stubbornly. 'If you wish me to stay behind, you will have to tie me up.'

'You red-headed vixen!' he exclaimed. 'You will do as I say.'

To prevent any further argument I swept to the open door and across the hall, only to be stopped at the entrance to the passageway by a hard hand on my arm. Furious, I swung round to face him.

'Let us settle it now!' I cried. 'I *will* go. I want to have it finished with.'

His mouth was set grimly. 'Very well. But you are to stay behind me, away from him. He will not be in the best of tempers.'

'I know. That's why I'm coming with you.'

Together, Ethan staying one pace ahead of me, we walked from the house. The dogs were chained to a post in the yard, the gates stood open. Beyond them, Piers sat his stallion. As we approached I could see the thunder-struck look of disbelief on his face.

164

'Georgiana!' he breathed. 'How ... My God, Marriott, if you've hurt her ...'

'I have not touched her,' Ethan said. 'See for yourself. But I have told her a great deal. She will not marry you, Cheviot.'

Piers turned to me, throwing out an appealing hand. 'He's lying, Georgiana. He has always hated me. He will stoop to any depths to wound me. Whatever he's told you, it is not true.'

'I think it is,' I said, running into Ethan's extended arm as I attempted to step forward. 'You were the one who lied to me. You have proved it by coming here. Everything is ended between us, Piers.'

The blood welled back into his face, making it dark with fury. 'You have betrayed me. And for him! For the murderer of Sophie. You will both pay for this!'

With a vicious twist of his hands he wrenched the stallion round and touched spurs to it. We watched him go a short distance and then we turned away, to walk slowly back to the house.

'Are you satisfied?' I asked.

Ethan smiled wryly. 'I have heard it said that revenge is sweet, but this one seems to have lost its savour. But I will bother with him no more. At least you are free of him. I cannot hope to protect the entire female population of these islands. They must ...'

At the same moment we both realized that

165

the hoofbeats were not drawing away but coming closer. I swung round in alarm as Piers rode full tilt through the gateway. Something gleamed in his hand. With a wordless cry Ethan pulled me round, protecting me with his own body. I heard a shot. Felt Ethan lurch, begin to fall. And then Piers was on me, sweeping me up in one arm and throwing me across the stallion's shoulders.

As he pulled the horse round to charge back towards the gate I had a glimpse of Ethan Marriott lying on his face on the cobbles, with blood staining his coat.

CHAPTER ELEVEN

Piers must have hit me when I struggled, for after that terrible sight in the yard I remember nothing until I slowly regained consciousness and found myself still draped uncomfortably in front of the saddle. A red mist stained my sight and I felt sick, too weak to do anything other than lie and endure the torture.

Eventually, after an indeterminable interval, the jolting stopped. Piers dismounted and lifted me down, dropping me onto the muddy ground as though I were a sack of potatoes.

I struggled to sit up, wiping my eyes. My hand came away wet with blood and further exploration told me that the gash in my head had opened and was bleeding freely.

'So you're awake.' Piers bent and jerked me to my feet. 'I did not want to hurt you, Georgiana. Perhaps now you will listen to reason.'

I was swaying where I stood, the blood running down my face, dripping from my chin. We were on the moors, I saw hazily, in a sunlit hollow beside a hut fashioned of grey stone.

Piers took my arm and dragged me towards the building, flinging open the rotting door. Sunlight filtered through a cobwebbed window that had no glass but only rough shutters. There was a table, two chairs, a stove, and a wide flat bench covered with a grimy blanket upon which Piers made me sit.

'Is this where you used to meet Jane Marriott?' I asked, staring at him dizzily.

A quiver passed over his face. For a moment he was about to repeat his denials, then he threw out his arms, saying passionately, 'Yes. Yes, I met her here. I told you there were things in my past that I regretted. Jane was beautiful, and lonely. She hated that forsaken house. But Marriott must take the blame, too. He has told you only his side of it. He would make it sound very bad, I know. He hated me.'

Hated. The past tense. Ethan . . .

'How did he get you to Wierdmoor House?' Piers demanded.

'You yourself put me into his own coach.

And I was afraid. Did you think of that when you decided to use me?'

'I did not mean you to come to harm!' he exclaimed angrily. 'I wanted only to stop him from annoying me further. But I ...' he paused, blue eyes filling with excitement. 'It may still come right for us. We can explain everything. He abducted you, and I shot him when I came to rescue you.'

'But you did not know I was there,' I said wearily. He was still lying, twisting everything. 'For what purpose did you come to Wierdmoor House today?'

His face darkened. 'To kill him! To avenge Sophie. I told them I had remembered someone who might fit the description of the Wolf. You see, it is all explained. We can go back and ...'

'But you killed an innocent man!' I cried.

'No!' He shook his head violently. 'No, he was guilty. You know it. Everyone knows it ... Listen, Georgiana, all we have to do is tell them I rescued you and shot Sophie's murderer. Then all will be well. We can be married and live ...'

'Never! I could never marry you after what you have done—to Jane Marriott and now to Ethan. How long would it be before some other beautiful woman caught your eye?'

His face was changing, being transformed to ugliness. 'You spurn me?' he demanded. 'You? Who the devil are you to refuse the heir to

168

Moorhollow!' He grasped my arm and flung me to the floor, standing over me as I lay half-dazed. 'Very well. You have had your chance. When I am done you will be sorry. Get up! This time you will not deny me. There is no-one to hear your screams. No-one to come to your rescue . . . Get up!'

I leaned on one hand and looked up at him through my tumbled hair. 'Do what you will. But Ethan Marriott's servants know that . . .'

'Servants!' he repeated scornfully. 'Servants can be bribed, or frightened into silence. *You* are the only one who can say what happened today, and you will not be here. When I carry your poor ill-used body to Moorhollow there will be no-one to say that the Wolf did not do it, or that I did not shoot him for it. No-one! Now get on your feet!'

Painfully, I picked myself up, leaning against the wall for support. 'You're a coward, Piers. A vile, despicable coward. You shot Ethan in the back. They will see that.'

'Ethan is it?' he grated. 'You call him by his first name already? You slut! You whore! You have conspired with him against me.'

He hit me, across the face with the flat of his hand, and as I reeled from the blow he grasped the neck of my gown and ripped it to the waist. Only my chemise protected me from his eyes. I threw my arms about my body, knowing I did not have the strength to fight him.

169

Piers took hold of me and forced me across to the bench, hitting me again when I resisted. I fell backwards and lay there, lights flashing across my eyes. I could see a wild light on his face as he bent over me.

'You will be a great help,' he said, almost laughing in his savage excitement. 'Who will blame me for putting an end to the man who both murdered my step-mother and defiled my bride-to-be?'

'He did not!' I mumbled. 'Ethan is no murderer.'

'No, but only you and I know that. It is all working out very well.'

As he bent closer I threw myself round and lashed out with my feet, sending him sprawling. The door was not far away but I was dizzy and Piers grasped a handful of my skirt. The material ripped, swinging me round as he leaped to his feet, cursing me viciously.

He reached for me again and stopped, his hands clawing out, his face livid. From across the moor there came the baying of the wolfhounds, filling the crisp air with their fury.

Piers dragged me to the window, from where I could see all six of the dogs streaming down the hill towards the hut. And behind them came a man riding a black stallion.

'No!!' There was both fury and fear on Piers' face. He half-believed the legend he had helped to create.

He ran for the door and out, but his horse

170

must have been frightened by the approach of the dogs for it was backing away, tossing its head and jumping nervously, its eyes rolling. As I clung to the door-post, I saw Piers leap and grasp the reins. The dogs were coming closer. The horse danced in terror. Piers got one foot in the stirrup before the first dog leapt.

Stricken with horror, I saw Piers lash out at the dog. His hand slipped from the reins. He fell. The stallion reared and surged forward, galloped away, dragging Piers behind. He was helpless, tossed and buffeted . . .

A shrill whistle drew the chasing dogs away and as I turned numbly Ethan Marriott drew rein beside me and half-fell from the saddle. He was white with pain, shaking and sweating, but he threw an arm about me and held me close to him for a moment.

I was unable to think or speak. Nothing seemed real.

'Thank God!' he breathed. 'Thank God! I thought . . .' The words choked off as his knees buckled. He collapsed against me and I sat down, holding his head in my lap. The side of his coat was soaked with blood, his breathing so shallow that for a moment I thought it had stopped.

Once again I was alone on the moor with a badly-wounded human being, but this time there was no-one to go for help, only the dogs sniffing curiously round, whining pitifully as if wondering why their master lay so still.

What was I to do? I wondered frantically. I had no idea how far I was from any habitation, or in which direction I should go. Ethan lay heavily on me, his face composed and waxen, the eyelids translucent so that tiny veins showed through, perspiration beading his brow and lip. The ridge of scar tissue appeared purple against the dead whiteness of his face. But he lived. I slipped my hand beneath his coat and could feel his heart beat, slow and rhythmical but very faint.

A tear slid down my cheek and fell on his hair. I had never felt so helpless. What would be best—to leave him and try to find help, or wait in hopes that I could get him back onto his horse when he recovered consciousness—if he ever did?

Pulling myself together, I managed to roll him so that he lay prostrate on the ground. A strip torn from my skirt made a pad to protect his head and then I could explore the wound. But it was beyond my small skill. The bullet was still lodged in the fleshy part of his shoulder, though the bleeding had stopped. I did not care to tear his coat and shirt for the air was chill. I had begun to shiver myself. My gown hung in ribbons.

The only thing to do was to go for help, leaving the dogs on guard. I stood up, hurried to the hut, and fetched the filthy blanket from the bench. At least it would help to keep

172

Ethan warm.

And then, as I emerged from the rough building, I saw that my prayers had been answered. Coming down the slope, on an unwilling carriage horse, was Henry Thomas.

'I tried to stop him,' he said wretchedly. 'He wouldn't listen.'

Between us we managed to lift Ethan and balance him across his saddle, then I rode the carriage horse while Henry led the stallion. It was a slow, anguished journey that we made across the moors to Wierdmoor House.

*   *   *

Doctor Mackay was a thin, dour man with a white moustache and bristling sidewhiskers. He stood beside the desk in Ethan Marriott's study and addressed me solemnly.

'I'm a plain man, Miss Forrest, and I'm perplexed. Some strange tales are being told in the Over Marton district. They say a hooded figure rides the moors with a pack of wolves. It sounds like nonsense, but I have seen those dogs you keep. Tell me, who shot Mr Marriott? The matter will have to be reported.'

'I know. I shall report it myself now that I know Mr Marriott is safe. He *will* recover, won't he?'

'He should, with rest and care. He's a fortunate young man. You won't tell me who did it?'

'It's a long story, Dr Mackay, too complicated to explain.'

'Then may I send the constable to hear it?'

Officious man. Did he doubt my word?

'That will not be necessary, thank you,' I replied. 'I shall go myself to Moorhollow.'

He looked surprised. 'The Cheviots' house? Then . . .' His tone hardened. 'Is Mr Marriott the man known as the Wolf?'

'As I said,' I answered tartly, 'the explanation is long and complex. I shall give it to those who ought to hear it. That I promise you. Meanwhile, for Mr Marriott's sake, I beg you to repeat none of this conversation. There has been enough gossip based on half-truths and speculation.'

'Very well,' he agreed sourly. 'I shall abide by your wishes. For the present. Good day, Miss Forrest.'

*   *   *

I wanted to stay at Wierdmoor House until Ethan awoke. And I was in need of rest myself. My head hurt and there were bruises and scratches all over my body, but as Piers had said, I was the only one who could tell what had occurred and there were still mysteries to be unravelled. It was my duty to go to Moorhollow.

Neither Henry nor Mrs Thomas were

anxious to let me go, but I convinced them it was the only thing to do. My only danger might come from Piers, but even if he had survived that last terrible journey he would be in no condition to do me more physical harm.

However, as Henry was preparing the gig his son rode into the yard—young Fred, the stable lad from Moorhollow—and told us that when Piers' stallion arrived home riderless a party had gone out to search the moor and had found Piers' mangled body. Fred had been a member of the group, but had left them to bring the news to Ethan Marriott. Piers Cheviot was dead.

'There'll be a great to-do,' the lad added. 'Mr Piers left this morning saying that he had an idea who the Wolf might be and was going to find out, and just after he'd gone a gentleman arrived from London. An inspector of police. Him and the constable have been asking hundreds of questions all morning.'

So Piers was dead. I felt no shame at being glad of it.

It was decided that Fred should return with me to Moorhollow. He knew the moors and could guide me, that being a much quicker route than the road. Since Ethan's stallion was the only real saddle-horse in the stables he was brought out again and Henry helped me mount.

We had been riding at a gentle canter for nearly an hour before I recognized on the skyline the big block of stone towards which Lucinda and I had raced. From there on I could have found my own way across the rolling hills and down into the valley.

The big, ugly house was quiet. When I rang the bell the housekeeper answered, her face tear-streaked.

'Miss Forrest! . . . Oh, ma'am, Mr Piers . . .'

'I know,' I said. 'Where is Mr Cheviot, Mrs Dewiss?'

'In the library, with the police Inspector from London. But he said I wasn't to disturb them.'

'I shall go on my own, if you don't mind.'

How familiar the house was, and how I detested it. Memories of Piers were everywhere—in the hall, the corridor, the library . . .

Taking a deep breath, I knocked on the library door.

*   *   *

It was fortunate that Mr Cheviot knew me to be a truthful person, for I had no means of proving what I had to say beyond producing Piers' pistol, which he had dropped in the yard of Wierdmoor House when he swept me onto his horse. The bruises which were now so evident on my face might have been caused by anyone, and there was only my word for the manner in which Piers had fallen from his horse.

'You say that Mr Piers Cheviot knew the identity of the Wolf the entire time?' the rotund Inspector asked sceptically.

'He did. Mr Marriott has a letter sent to his wife by Piers. When he is well enough he will confirm what I have said.'

It was clear that Mr Cheviot could not take in all of this new information. He said, 'If Piers knew, why did he not say so?'

'He couldn't,' I said. 'He did not want you to know what he had done to Jane Marriott. I'm sorry to bring you added grief, but Ethan Marriott's name must be cleared. He did not kill Sophie. He was away in York on the night she died, and Piers ...' I could not bear to watch him, so turned instead to the Inspector, 'Piers knew who the murderer was. He told me as much. In the end, that was why he had to kill me. He did not know that Ethan Marriott was still alive and could provide an alibi. He said ... He said, "Only you and I know that Ethan Marriott is not the murderer. It is all working out very well." '

'Only you and he?' the Inspector repeated. 'Are you implying that he confessed to the murder?'

My throat felt thick and my eyes stung, not for Piers but for his family.

'That was how it seemed to me,' I said in a husky voice.

'No!' Mr Cheviot leaped to his feet. 'You

must be mistaken. Why should my son . . .' He stopped abruptly, as if he had remembered something.

'He did not tell me why,' I said. 'At the time I was too afraid to think clearly. But I'm sure that is what he meant. That is why he came to kill Ethan Marriott, so that no-one would ever guess the truth. If I had not been there it might have happened as he planned and everyone would have believed Ethan Marriott to be a murderer. Piers would have gone free.'

Mr Cheviot was standing like a man turned to stone, his face working. He sat down abruptly, staring into the distance.

'Dear God!' he got out. 'Dear God, she must have lied to me.'

'Who lied, sir?' the Inspector asked gently.

'My wife! It must be. My wife . . . and my son. I saw him leaving her room one night. She told me some tale about a secret gift she was buying for me with Piers' help. I wanted to believe her. I didn't want to think that . . .'

'What's that maid's name?' the Inspector barked at me. 'The French one?'

'Babette?'

'That's the one. Send someone to fetch her.'

Babette came, looking grim and determined for some reason, and I was dismissed from the library.

I found Annalie and Lucinda in the drawing-room, both of them wearing deep mourning, as they had done before I left.

'Georgiana!' Annalie flung herself into my arms, weeping. 'Oh, it's too awful. First Sophie and now Piers.'

'What are you doing here?' Lucinda asked dully.

'It's too long a story to tell now,' I replied. 'I want your help. Both of you.'

'Help?' Annalie raised a wet face, blinking, then said, 'Oh, your face . . .'

'You look as though someone has beaten you,' Lucinda added.

'Yes, someone did. But will you both please try to think. Do you remember what was found in Sophie's hand?'

'Silver braid on black cloth,' Lucinda said.

'From the Wolf's burnous,' Annalie amplified.

'No. Not from the Wolf. From something in this house. Think hard. Have you ever seen anything like that here?'

'Never,' Lucinda said at once.

Annalie looked bewildered. 'I don't think so. But it *was* the Wolf, Georgiana. Why do you say . . .'

'I have met the Wolf. I have been staying at his house. His burnous is all in one piece and he was away in York that night.'

Lucinda's eyes flared wide as she stared at me. 'Then I was right. You are in league with him!'

'I am now!' I cried impatiently. 'He is innocent. Even the police believe that after

179

what I have been able to tell them, and there is the proof to be had if they need it ... Please, think about the piece of braid. Where could it be from?'

'Well ...' Annalie said slowly, frowning, 'now that I think about it ... I do seem to remember a ... a uniform, that Piers wore once to a costume ball. It was black and silver. But it has been stored away in the attic for years.'

'Where? Can you show me?'

She led the way to the very top of the house, to a room full of old furniture, pictures and trunks. We searched two of the trunks before we found, rolled up at the bottom in a piece of sacking, the black Hussar's uniform with the silver frogging. One of the fastenings had been torn out of it.

'No!' Annalie breathed. 'Not someone at Moorhollow!'

'I'm afraid so, Annalie. Let us take this to the Inspector.'

*　　　*　　　*

The mystery was resolved after many questions and much explaining. On coming to England with her elderly husband, Sophie had fallen passionately in love with her handsome step-son. Piers, being what he was, had not hesitated long before giving in to the pull of a mutual desire. Sophie had been able to cajole

Mr Cheviot and allay all his suspicions, but the lovers had needed a go-between and had employed Babette.

The Inspector, shrewder than he looked, had understood this possibility. When questioned, Babette confessed that she had known of the affair, had helped them and kept watch for them. From Sophie she had learned everything that was said. Sophie, of course, would have enjoyed talking about her conquest.

Piers had told her about his problem with Ethan Marriott and they had agreed that he should find a suitable woman, engage himself to her, and let the Wolf do what he wished. He could then be arrested and imprisoned, out of Piers' way.

What neither of them had foreseen was that Piers' fickle affections would turn in my direction. I hesitate to call the emotion love. He had desired me and would no doubt have tired quickly after his lust was satisfied. But Sophie had understood that she was losing her hold on him, even though the child she carried might well have been fathered by Piers. She had threatened to tell her husband the truth, which would have meant disgrace for them both and disinheritance for Piers. He could not live with the thought of losing his fortune, but Sophie would always have him in her power, while she lived. And so he killed her.

Babette, knowing the lovers had quarrelled,

came eventually, in her slow-witted way, to wonder if Piers had killed his mistress. She mentioned it to him and he gave her a gold bracelet to keep quiet, also threatening her with a similar fate if she dared say anything. But now that Piers was dead she gladly brought forth her accusations and doubts.

It was a sordid tale of betrayal, unspeakable in its iniquity. And to think I once fancied myself in love with Piers and a friend of Sophie. I understood now a good many of her barbed remarks and unreadable glances. Sophie had been playing with me until she began to hate me, and she had been only too eager to encourage Lucinda's antipathy, in the hope that I would be smeared by the lies.

The Inspector was prepared to overlook the personal feud between Ethan Marriott and Piers since Ethan had not broken any written laws. It was no crime to wear unusual garments, or keep a pack of wolfhounds, or ride abroad by moonlight. His only actual wrongdoing had been the abducting of one Miss Georgiana Forrest, but the lady concerned was not prepared to bring charges on that account.

As it was late evening by the time the enquiries were closed, Mr Cheviot insisted that I should sleep in my old room at Moorhollow. In some ways his bitterness over his betrayal by his wife and son had served to strengthen him, though I feared it would make him a harsher man.

I spent a restless night worrying about Ethan Marriott and in the morning hurried through a light breakfast.

'Are you going back there?' Annalie asked as she followed me out of the house, her face wan against the black gown. 'Back to the Wolf?'

'The Wolf no longer exists,' I said gently. 'He is Ethan Marriott and that is all. And he's very ill, Annalie. I would not have left him if I had not been the only one left to tell the truth of what happened.'

Annalie was watching Fred bring up the horses. He was returning to Wierdmoor House with me.

'Oh . . .' Annalie gasped. 'That's *his* horse. He's so huge! Are you sure you can manage him?'

Lucinda's voice came from the doorway. 'Of course she can. She's an excellent horsewoman.'

Her face told me nothing, but I guessed it was the nearest she could come to an apology. We would never be friends.

I stepped into Fred's waiting hands and settled myself on the black stallion, bidding them goodbye. Before they were out of sight I glanced back and saw that Lucinda had her arm about Annalie in a gesture of sisterly comfort. It was the one good thing to come of the whole tragic affair.

183

'Thank the good lord you've come back,' Mrs Thomas greeted me. 'I haven't known what to do with the master. First of all he was trying to get up and come after you, then when I told him young Mr Cheviot wouldn't bother neither of you no more he started to watch the clock. He was certain you'd be back by dark. He won't eat nor talk, just lies there staring into space. When you didn't come home last night he thought you'd gone for good . . . You better go and see him, miss. He won't take no notice of me. And will you try and make him have some of this broth?'

Throwing off my hat and gloves, I hurried up the stairs, taking with me a bowl of hot broth.

Ethan was lying propped up by pillows, a bandage bound round his naked shoulder and chest. I could not see his face clearly for the curtains were still pulled across the window and only the fire gave light to the room.

'What's this?' I said briskly, going straightaway to the window. 'The sun is shining and you lie here in the gloom.'

As I threw back the curtains the sunlight poured in. I could see it glinting on the rippling waves in the bay below.

'Why did you go there?' Ethan demanded, keeping his face turned away from me.

184

'I had to,' I said quietly. 'I had to explain everything to them and clear your name. Piers told me a great deal. It was he who killed Sophie.'

His head snapped round, the movement bringing a spasm of pain to his face. 'He did? Why?'

'I'll tell you all about it—if you will take some of this broth.'

He glared at me fiercely but did not protest as I sat beside and began to feed him, a spoonful at a time. Soon the bowl was empty.

'Now you tell me,' he ordered, fastening his hand around my arm so that I could not get up.

It did not take long in the telling, for he already knew most of the story. When I had finished he no longer looked fierce but only weary.

'Did you really think I would desert you?' I asked. 'I know you have only Mrs Thomas to look after you. She cannot be expected to cope with everything.'

'Then you'll stay?' he said hopefully.

'Until you are well again, if I may.' That was the limit to which I dared go. When he was recovered there would be no excuse for me to remain at Wierdmoor House.

As the days went by, Ethan gradually regained his strength. I sat with him for hours, reading to him, playing chess, or simply talking with him. Soon he was fit enough to work on his accounts and write business letters to make sure his affairs were kept in order. He did not seem anxious to leave his bed, but after three weeks Mrs Thomas and I persuaded him down to the drawing-room, which we had swept and dusted and polished to new life.

On a crisp November day we went walking down to the beach, with the dogs. Ethan was well again, I knew. He still kept his right arm in a sling, but apart from that he had resumed a normal life. It was time for me to be leaving. More than time. Only my own selfish reluctance to be parted from him was keeping me at Wierdmoor House.

He threw a stick far out across the rocks and the dogs went joyfully leaping for it.

Clearing my throat nervously, I said, 'When will there be a stage-coach for London?'

Ethan looked round, the laughter dying from his face and being replaced by a look of blank stillness.

'In two days time, I believe. But there is no hurry. You said you would stay until I was recovered.'

'You *are* recovered.' Unable to look at him, I watched the dogs fighting over the stick. 'It is time I was leaving.'

'Of course,' he said flatly. 'If you want to go, you must.'

'It is not a question of what I want, but what is right. I have no right to be here, imposing on your hospitality. I must begin to make plans for the future, find some employment. You will agree that my position here is somewhat unorthodox.'

'Does it matter?'

'It does to me.'

I heard him sigh heavily. 'If that is the case then I need no longer keep up the charade.'

Puzzled, I glanced round. I saw him take off the sling, flexing his shoulder and arm and affording me one of his wry smiles.

'I'm a fraud, Georgiana. The wound was healed some time ago, but I asked Mrs Thomas not to tell you. I have been deliberately prolonging my illness. I wanted to keep you here as long as I could.'

'Why?'

'Why?' Ethan laughed bitterly. 'Because I do not relish the thought of being alone again, without you. I had to use subterfuge. What else would have kept you here? I am not a rich man, and even if I were my wealth would not compensate you for living with a man who looks like a monster.'

'You do not!' I exclaimed angrily. 'You will ruin your life if you do not forget that scar.'

'Could *you* forget it?'

'I had already done so until you mentioned it. It's such a tiny part of you. It's your character I think of. The person you are.'

'Is it?' He took my face between his hands and forced me to look at him squarely. 'But what do you see when you look at me?'

'A man,' I said, throwing caution to the winds. 'A man who is tall and strong, who can be fierce or gentle. A courageous man who risked his own life to save mine. A man I . . .' My voice fell to a whisper and I closed my eyes tightly against the tears that pricked them. 'A man I love beyond all reason.'

There was a moment of complete silence.

'Georgiana,' he said wonderingly. 'Georgiana. You love me?'

'I do.'

'Then I will not let you leave,' he asserted, taking me in his arms. 'I have loved you from the first time we met. In the lane outside Moorhollow. Do you remember?'

I looked up into dark eyes that were suddenly full of tenderness and I knew why I had never completely trusted Piers. He had never looked at me in that way, nor had I felt then the tenth part of what I felt now.

'How could I ever forget it?' I said, laughing.

'Georgiana.' He seemed to like saying my name. 'Georgiana, my dearest love . . .'

Shortly after this we returned to the house to tell Mrs Thomas the glad news. Never again need I fear a grey, empty life as a spinster teacher. I was going to be the wife of the Wolf of Wierdmoor.